WITCHROCK

Other books by Bill Knox available from New English Library:

STORMTIDE
WHITEWATER
HELLSPOUT

WITCHROCK

Bill Knox

NEW ENGLISH LIBRARY/TIMES MIRROR

For David and Elizabeth

First published in Great Britain in 1977 by John Long Ltd, an imprint of the Hutchinson Publishing Group

First NEL Paperback Edition June 1979

NEL Books are published by
New English Library from
Barnard's Inn, Holborn,
London EC1N 2JR.
Made and printed in Great Britain by
C. Nicholls & Company Ltd.,
The Philips Park Press, Manchester

45004252 9

PRELUDE

George MacKenzie came back to reality slowly, feeling sick and confused, not knowing where he was or how he'd got there. But his fingers told him that he was lying on cold, hard, strangely damp rock. He could hear the steady rhythm of breaking waves somewhere very near, and the air had a salty tang.

He stirred, giving a soft moan at the effort it cost him. The movement brought a raucous, indignant screech followed by a quick flapping of wings. Startled, he forced his eyes open and raised his head.

It was night. The moon was almost obscured by cloud but there was enough light to show the white shape of a large herring gull circling watchfully a few feet above him. He was lying on black, smooth-worn rock close to the sea and a lighthouse was flashing steadily somewhere out across the water.

A tall but thin man, with greying hair and a leathery skin, MacKenzie let his face fall against the cold rock again and lay still, breathing in short gasps while he began to remember.

It had been close to midnight, with the tide well on the ebb, and he'd taken his boat out into the Brannan Sound for a couple of hours of line-fishing.

Low tide and slack water was the best time for fishing in the Sound – and fishing had always been his favourite method of getting away from the rest of the world when he had to think his way through a problem.

From there, suddenly, he remembered the rest with a frightening clarity. The other, bigger boat that had loomed out of the night and come alongside. The two men who had jumped aboard, the gun that had been pointed at him, the flicker of movement he'd caught out of the corner of his eye, a prelude to oblivion as something blunt and hard had been brought down on his head. His head still ached and throbbed where it had happened.

Determinedly forcing his body to obey, George MacKenzie managed to get to his hands and knees. He stayed that way for a minute, shivering despite the heavy fisherman-knit wool sweater he wore with old blue serge trousers, thick socks and the down-at-heel seaboots he'd cut to ankle length.

Inquisitive, the gull swooped down. Its wings almost brushed him as it passed and the big, cruel beak opened in another shrill cry. He swore at it, heaved himself upright, and stood swaying on his feet. Head thumping, he looked around, saw why the waves were breaking so close to him, and knew raw, clutching fear.

He was on a low, time-worn natural platform of rock which had the sea all around it. Pock-marked here and there by tiny tidal pools, totally flat and empty, a black, wet gleam in the faint moonlight, the rock wasn't more than thirty feet across at its widest point. And the distant lighthouse with its steady flashing stood on a dark mass of headland which made everything else unmistakable.

He was on the Witchrock, the most dreaded spot in the Brannan Sound, a finger of black basalt rock covered by a full seven feet of water when the tide was full, only drying out and visible when the sea retreated to the half-tide mark or less. Five miles away across the Sound, the flashing light on Broch Point marked the nearest land.

Little things suddenly and irrationally mattered to George MacKenzie. He discovered his clothes were only damp, not wet, that his wristwatch had gone but that his cigarettes and lighter were still in his hip pocket. He noticed the way a long strand of dark kelpweed had been left snagged to a crack in the rock near his feet. Then realization came home to him again.

God, he was on the Witchrock. He brought out his cigarettes, lit one with hands that quivered, and tried to work out time and tide.

At most, he reckoned, he had a couple of hours.

Wings fluttered and he looked round again. The gull had landed nearby and was eyeing him insolently, no longer afraid. But it rose again as a wave larger than the rest broke white and came swirling in, to lap against MacKenzie's feet.

Moistening his salt-dried lips, he dropped the stub of his cigarette. The red tip died with a hiss then the tiny stub was drawn away as the water retreated.

And MacKenzie tensed as a new sound reached his ears, the faint murmur of an engine. The murmur grew until, straining his eyes against the night, he picked out the silhouette of an approaching boat. It came on slowly, without lights, the soft, thudding beat of its engine a monotonous rhythm, a mere wisp of phosphorescent wake showing astern as it started to circle the gradually shrinking patch of black rock.

George MacKenzie shouted and waved and dragged out his cigarette lighter, sparking it to life and moving the tiny flame frantically above his head.

The boat came nearer, still circling. But suddenly MacKenzie knew it for what it was and let his arms fall despairingly to his sides.

They had come back to make sure. As if to confirm it, the boat began to widen the circle again, her engine beat now reduced to a point where it could be giving little more than steerage way.

The next wave to foam in across the rock snatched at MacKenzie's ankles and the next did the same, while he cursed the men who were out there, watching and waiting.

The darkened boat kept to its slow, wide circles while the tide crept in. The wavecrests were slapping at his knees and the entire black hump of the Witchrock had been swallowed back by the sea when George MacKenzie decided he had had enough.

He was no swimmer, but he had no choice – unless he wanted to just stand and wait for death.

He had already kicked off his seaboots. Now he pulled off his heavy sweater, threw it aside, and deliberately began walking into the waves. When he reached chest-height he stopped and saw the boat murmuring in a little closer, as if the crew's curiosity had been roused.

'Damn you all to hell,' he shouted, and began swimming.

It was five miles to the headland, against the tidal stream. George MacKenzie was tired after ten minutes, exhausted after fifteen. He struggled on a little longer, using a clumsy breast-stroke. Then he simply sank from sight.

The boat nosed in near to where he'd gone down. Men hustled briefly on deck and George MacKenzie's dinghy was dumped over the side, overturned. A boat-hook shoved it clear, then the boat gathered speed and turned away. To the east, the sky beyond Broch Point was beginning to grey with the first hint of early dawn.

Far below, a school of young mullet scattered in the underwater darkness as the strange, lifeless shape sank down, limbs still twitching occasionally in the pull of an unseen current.

Lower down, where the bottom weed waited, the dead man's body snagged briefly on a ridge of rock. The current pressed impatiently and he came free again, rolling grotesquely.

In the process, a slip of plastic fell from his hip pocket. It drifted down and landed on soft sand, sending a startled fiddler crab scuttling away.

The plastic card said that Constable George MacKenzie was an officer of the Scottish Northern Constabulary and showed his photograph. The little fiddler crab crawled over the warrant card a moment later, then the first grains of sand began to settle in.

CHAPTER ONE

The pale January sun shone down on a cold, grey Edinburgh which was shivering under a wind from the north. Snow was forecast, most of the population seemed to have gone into hibernation, and the few off-season tourists bravely exploring Princes Street were discovering why their package tours had been low-cost.

It was even colder up on Calton Hill, where the wind whipped the flags which flew above the austere frontage of St Andrews House, central government administration headquarters for Scotland. Outside the building, sitting behind the wheel of a parked station wagon, Chief Officer Webb Carrick of Her Majesty's Fishery Protection cruiser *Marlin* kept his feet under the stream of lukewarm air being churned out by the heater fan and watched the rear-view mirror. He had it angled so that he could see the massive bronze doors of the main entrance without turning round.

His broad-boned, weather-bronzed face shaped a grin as a girl in a sheepskin coat and knee-length boots scurried out, crossed the parking lot, and tumbled into one of the cars as if frostbite was nipping at her high heels. Then, behind her, another figure emerged from the building, the one he'd been waiting on.

Small, plump and bearded, like an elderly teddy bear in a duffel coat, Captain James Shannon stumped his way across to the station wagon, got in on the passenger side, and slammed the door shut with a grunt.

'Blasted bureaucratic beehive,' said Shannon bitterly. Hunched in the seat, he chewed a stray tendril of beard for a moment. 'Ever notice what's carved on the doors, mister?'

Cautiously, Carrick merely nodded while his gaze strayed back to the rear-view mirror. The Biblical quotation 'Follow Me and Ye shall be Fishers of Men' was heavily embossed on the metal doors, the pious whim of an earlier, Calvinistic generation. It certainly had nothing to do with Fishery Protection – their headquarters base was on the other side of the city, at Leith Docks.

'I'll tell you what that mob in there are really saying,' grunted Shannon cynically. 'Hard luck, everybody – but we've got you on the hook.' He glared at the world outside the station wagon. 'The next patrol is cancelled. We're being detached for special duty, floating errand boys – when all they need for the job is any damned overgrown rowing boat.'

Carrick raised an eyebrow, but the way the summons had come meant he wasn't totally surprised. Four hundred tons of fast patrol cruiser and built like a miniature destroyer, *Marlin* was in harbour at Greenock, on the Clyde, which was over fifty miles away. Her crew had straggled back from a week's leave that morning and she was due to sail for the Outer Hebrides on the evening tide.

But Captain Shannon had had to drop everything when the message from St Andrews House had arrived. Then they'd come charging through, Carrick being brought along to chauffeur their borrowed Fishery Protection transport. Shannon would tackle any hazard afloat, but he was a nervous wreck on four wheels.

'What kind of special duty?' asked Carrick, realizing that the information wasn't going to be volunteered.

'Servants of democracy,' answered Shannon. His moon-shaped face shaped a new scowl. 'They're voting in the Lochard constituency Parliamentary by-election at the end of the week. It happened to include a whole damned clutch of off-shore islands –'

'And we've to ferry in the ballot boxes?' Carrick winced at the thought. Fishery cruisers got landed with that kind of job now and again. It meant dealing with fussy local officials, fussier party agents, and all the other fringe awkwardnesses of a political circus. 'Where will we base, sir?'

'Feanport – it's a fishing village on the mainland, near the head of the Brannon Sound.' Shannon glanced at his wristwatch, sucked his lips thoughtfully, then asked, 'Did you get that spares list problem sorted out?'

'Yes, sir.' Carrick nodded solemnly. The spares list problem was the kind created by Shannon for Shannon – an excuse to get Carrick along as driver. 'I saw our Department people. It's straightened out.' He paused, then added tentatively, 'If we're finished here, maybe we could eat before we head back west. I know a place –'

'Here, in Edinburgh?' Shannon looked startled at the

thought. 'Mister, I haven't that kind of time to waste. More important, I know what they charge for a drink. No, just get moving – we'll eat aboard *Marlin*.'

'Aboard *Marlin*,' agreed Carrick sadly. He key-started the station wagon, began backing it out, and asked over his shoulder, 'Why did we draw the ballot-box run?'

'Simple,' grated Shannon. 'Every other Fishery Protection captain on the west coast has gone into hiding, has engine trouble aboard or has dreamed up an excuse. They wouldn't have caught me if we hadn't been coming back from leave.' He paused, watching nervously as they left the parking lot and slipped smoothly into the main road's traffic stream. Then, relaxing with a sigh, he asked, 'Ever been to Feanport, mister?'

Carrick shook his head, keeping his attention ahead.

'The average fisherman around Feanport could give a mule lessons on being stubborn.' Shannon kept silent for a moment as they passed a perfectly harmless truck then drew a relieved breath. 'Still, there's one particular claim it has to fame. Ever met a real, live witch, mister?'

'There's a few of them around,' said Carrick mildly. 'Blonde, brunette and redhead – I'm not prejudiced.'

'Very funny,' said Shannon sourly. 'But don't expect a laugh from it around Feanport. There's a woman up there called the Witch of the Isles and the average skipper around the Brannan Sound still makes sure he keeps on her good side. A few even ask her blessing on their boats at the start of a season.'

'Suppose the by-election candidates get the same idea?' asked Carrick, unrepentant and the hungry drive ahead still annoying him. 'Sort of play Cinderella and say they want to go to Parliament.'

'Turn pumpkins into politicians?' Shannon gave a humourless grunt. 'I think somebody's been doing it for a long time.' Then he settled deeper in his seat and half-closed his eyes. 'I'm going to catch some sleep, mister. So stop yapping and watch your driving. I'm getting too near pension age to take risks.'

The weather forecast had been right. The first flecks of snow began falling almost as he spoke.

By dawn the next morning the fishery cruiser *Marlin* had travelled a long way from the Clyde. Her lean grey hull was thrusting through lumping seas in the Passage of Tiree, the five-mile-wide channel that cuts a reef-fringed track towards the Outer Isles.

But it had been a long, hard night. She had sailed from Greenock on the evening tide straight into a blinding snowstorm, the kind that reduced visibility to a swirling obscurity. The snow had stayed with her, on and off, until almost three a.m. with Captain Shannon constantly in the command chair and refusing to compromise with the weather. While most other craft had been heading for shelter he had navigated by instinct as much as the radar screen – and *Marlin* had stayed on course and schedule.

'He's a stubborn old sod,' declared Petty Officer William 'Clapper' Bell with a wry admiration. Massive paws wrapped around a mug of galley coffee, newly relieved from the helm, he gave a tired-edged grin towards Webb Carrick, who had draped himself against one of the bridge heaters. 'You look the way I feel – knackered.'

'Who's arguing?' Carrick yawned, and braced himself as the fishery cruiser rolled and a new curtain of spray drenched her hundred-and-eighty-foot length.

Shannon had left them only minutes before, heading below to his day cabin. The sky had cleared overhead. To starboard, the high hills of Mull were a startling white with a red rim of watery sun gradually rising behind them. On ahead, twin pinpricks of light still stabbed a pale challenge at the dawn from the northern end of the Passage. But, as it had all night, the rest of the world seemed compounded of the steady, underfoot vibration of the fishery cruiser's twin diesels and the high-pitched singing of the wind through her aerial rigging.

'So what's the rush?' Clapper Bell, *Marlin*'s bo'sun and six feet of brawny, ginger-haired Irishman, ambled across to join him. 'Somebody stand on the Old Man's tail?'

'Something like that,' agreed Carrick mildly. Clapper Bell was his partner in the fishery cruiser's scuba-diving team and that kind of mutual reliance created its own kind of discipline. 'Don't expect too many happy smiles till we've collected those ballot boxes.'

'Playin' at ferry-boats for a few days won't harm him.' Bell's eyes were heavy from lack of sleep and he needed a shave badly. 'Anyway, there are worse places than Feanport.'

'If you know where the action is?' asked Carrick dryly.

'They've never even heard o' the word,' admitted Bell sadly. 'There's a stone-faced village cop called MacKenzie who makes sure o' that. But he's all right off duty – I got pretty friendly wi' him.' He fought back a yawn. 'Still, I'm wi' the Old Man on one thing. Stuff all politicians – an' I'm off to my pit while I still know how to get there.'

He left, clattering down the companionway stair that led aft. The new helmsman, a ruddy-faced native of Barra, was humming under his breath as he eased the wheel a fraction. The relief lookouts on the bridge wings were already slapping their arms and stamping their feet as they got used to the temperature, and Carrick was left as the last of the overnight watch still on duty.

Some tiny, moving dots caught his eye on the Mull shoreline. He lifted the bridge glasses, then gave a sympathetic grunt as the dots came into focus through the powerful lenses. They were deer, forced down from the hills by the ferocity of the overnight blizzard – and, at that, they were probably the lucky ones.

'Picture-postcard stuff,' said a cheerful young voice unexpectedly. 'That's what I call a view, Webb.'

'You're late.' Carrick lowered the glasses and scowled at the chubby, freckle-faced arrival. Jumbo Wills, the second mate, showed all the benefits of a few hours' sleep but Carrick was in no mood for bright-eyed vigour. 'Where the hell have you been?'

'Checking the weather forecast.' Wills looked slightly hurt. 'Wind decreasing, occasional light showers, moderate sea – and the temperature rising soon. No problems.'

'Right.' Thankfully, Carrick dumped the bridge glasses on their shelf. 'We're on zero-zero-nine magnetic and you have the watch.'

'Zero-zero-nine,' repeated Wills dutifully with a glance at the helmsman, who nodded. 'Anything else?'

'You've to call the Old Man when you clear Ardnamurchan Point,' Carrick told him.

'Why?' The last of Wills's smile faded.

'Ask him,' suggested Carrick, wooden-faced. Jumbo Wills had a sad record of minor disasters on most patrols and Captain Shannon tended to treat their second mate like a juvenile delinquent. 'But do it when he's in a happier mood.'

Flushing, Wills levered himself up into the command chair while another lumping sea sent *Marlin* rolling and fresh spume spattered against the bridge. Then he faced Carrick again.

'I'll tell you something people keep forgetting,' said Wills frostily. 'If you and the Old Man were both washed overboard or something equally beneficial, then I'd be left in command of this ship.'

'You'd want a band playing that day,' said Carrick sourly. 'One like they had on the *Titanic* when she went down.'

Wills spluttered. The helmsman made a choking noise and kept his eyes glued to the compass – and, satisfied, Carrick headed aft, past the tiny chartroom and down the first flight of companionway stairs.

He paused there, then from sheer habit opened a door and stepped out on to the lee side of the main deck to look around.

Even there, sheltered from the worst of the wind and spume, the cold cut like a knife. But *Marlin*'s duty watch were already settling into their daytime routine. Two oilskin-clad ratings were methodically checking their way along the lashings on the deck gear. He could hear the coughing rasp of a launch engine being started on test and further aft, past the pulsing shimmer of exhaust throbbing from *Marlin*'s squat funnel, a figure was dumping trash from the galley over the side while the usual attendant gulls swooped in.

Tired as he was, Carrick stayed a moment longer watching the gulls then the way that the Blue Ensign of the fishery protection squadron flapped and crackled at *Marlin*'s stern. But he was still glad to step back into the warmth, close the door, and head 'tween decks and aft.

Andy Shaw, their chief engineer, was finishing breakfast alone in the wardroom. A lanky, middle-aged individual who always looked grimy, Shaw gave him a yawning nod but left it at that. Like Carrick, he'd been on watch through the night.

'Coffee and a bacon sandwich – I'll take them with me,' Carrick told the hovering steward. While he waited, he turned to Shaw. 'Good leave?'

'What I can remember of it,' said Shaw dolefully. 'Want to buy what's left of a hangover? Last night was one hell of a way to try to cure it.'

Carrick grinned in sympathy, collected his mug of coffee

and the thick slab of sandwich, and went along the narrow passage which led to his cabin. Going in, he heeled the door shut behind him, sat down on the edge of the narrow bunk with a sigh of relief, and chewed on the sandwich without really tasting it.

Thirty-one years of age, stocky, five-foot-ten in height, with the kind of muscular shoulders which came from keeping in constant scuba-diving trim, Webb Carrick had been chief officer aboard *Marlin* for a shade more than two years. He had dark brown eyes, darker brown hair and a broad-boned face with lips a little too thin to allow any idea that an easy-going manner meant he could be pushed around – as even Captain Shannon had learned.

Most of the tiny crow's-foot lines around his eyes had been acquired in those last two years while *Marlin* patrolled the treacherous, island-studded Scottish west coast. There had been plenty to learn, from a new, fine-honed brand of seamanship to the realities of keeping the peace and maintaining the law in the multi-million-pound Scottish fishing industry.

Marlin rolled again. Carrick swore to himself as some of the coffee slopped from the mug. Then he gulped down the rest and abandoned the bacon sandwich, realizing he'd been almost asleep.

All he really wanted to do was to get his head down. Stripping off his uniform jacket and the white roll-neck sweater he wore under it, he kicked off his short-length seaboots and crossed the cabin to splash some water on his face at the tiny washbasin. Drying off with a towel which caught at his dark beard stubble, he finished undressing, flopped down on the bunk, and considered the cabin through heavy eyes,

It was small and sparsely furnished, the single port-hole close to the waterline, any extras he'd added being bachelor-style from the few books crammed into a shelf to a framed photograph of his last ship, a deep-sea oil tanker.

That seemed another life away, one that had ended when, a newly won master's ticket in his pocket but no ship available, he'd been called to Fisheries Department interview on the strength of a long-forgotten application. The same day he'd been appointed chief officer under Shannon and had been handed the black warrant card which declared Webster Carrick an assistant Superintendent of Fisheries.

A hybrid mixture of sea-going policeman and civil servant with, from the average fisherman's viewpoint, the worst features of both.

Fishermen were supposed to work within rules and quotas, seasonal bans, net sizes, zones and limits, even Common Market regulations in the modern mood. Boats of a dozen nationalities could be found fishing off the Scottish coastline – and German or Dutch, French, Russian or native Scot, they shared a stubborn, independent streak and a basic code.

Get the fish, and you get the money. The local Scottish boats on their own landed a regular £60 million worth of catch at Scottish ports.

With maybe a quarter of it caught illegally, according to some market men. Lying back, Carrick listened to the steady throb of *Marlin*'s engines and the sound of the seas which met her hull.

Like the rest of the protection flotilla, she covered an average of 17,000 sea miles a year on her beat from the Butt of Lewis in the north to the southern limits of the Solway.

Keeping the lid on things. Chasing poachers through all weathers and among a maze of islands, reefs and currents which had few parallels anywhere. Or, suddenly, having to switch to any one of a score of other roles from rescue to settling local fishing wars or plain law enforcement.

He yawned, eyes almost closed, thinking of Shannon and the other protection cruiser skippers who had to outwit and outsail the fishermen at their own game among the islands.

That needed a tight, efficient ship – the way Shannon ran *Marlin*. No guns broke the line of her distinctive silhouette of high-raked bow and square cut stern. What she had instead was the thirty-knot speed of her twin 2,000 horsepower diesels, the Blue Ensign with the gold Fisheries badge, and her go-anywhere capability.

Which came back to Shannon again, with his crew of twenty, three watch-keeping officers and an armoury of cunning.

The kind of cunning learned the hard way that Carrick knew Shannon was now trying to pass on to him – pass on in the short time left before Captain James Shannon reached compulsory retirement age and was pensioned off like some old, abandoned horse – which in itself was a hell of a thought and a hell of a waste. Except, decided Carrick as his eyes finally closed, Shannon would fight that day off as long as he could – with the same kind of cunning.

The sea had moderated. It was the first thing that registered with Webb Carrick when he wakened. The fishery cruiser's pitching roll had become an easy, gentle sway and though her engine beat was unchanged there was no longer spray washing across his cabin porthole.

Even better, the sky outside was a bright, cloudless blue. It was noon by his wristwatch, which surprised him and meant he'd been asleep for almost six hours. Yawning, he got out of the bunk and reached for the shelf where he kept his cigarettes.

Then he remembered and swore sadly. The last pack of cigarettes he'd bought was firmly taped above the wash-basin mirror, still unopened. He'd promised himself this trip was the one on which he was going to kick the habit.

Try anyway. Gloomily, he washed and shaved, finished dressing, then ambled back to the porthole. The weather had certainly cleared and from the distant coastline's shape *Marlin* had come another long way while he'd slept.

A few minutes later he went up to the bridge. It was bathed in bright sunlight, the helmsman was wearing sun glasses to cut down the glare, and the officer of the watch was now Ferguson, a thin, grey-haired figure who grunted a greeting.

'Who bribed the weather man?' asked Carrick cheerfully, looking around. They were about three miles off the mainland, a long line of low green hills untouched by white. Ahead, a small cluster of islands basked in the sunlight on the port bow and he could just make out a string of tiny line-fishing boats working close in to their rock-fringed shores. 'Whatever it cost, I'll pay my share.'

'If you mean what happened to the snow, we left that behind when we cleared Skye,' said Ferguson in a flat, disinterested voice.

Ferguson was middle-aged, *Marlin*'s third watch-keeping officer, and a withdrawn man. He rated junior second mate and had returned to sea after a long interval ashore – though exactly why he'd returned was a reason he kept to himself. As he spoke, he strode across to the compass binnacle, frowned suspiciously, then sniffed.

'Starboard a point, helmsman,' he ordered curtly. 'You're damned well daydreaming again.'

'Starboard, sir.' The helmsman obeyed then added something softly under his breath as Ferguson turned away. *Marlin*'s junior second didn't top the ship's popularity poll. There was a big basking shark travelling almost parallel with them to port, its tall, black, sail-like fin cutting through the swell – but the helmsman reckoned it wouldn't have liked Ferguson either.

'Tell me something,' said Ferguson, grimacing as he came back to join Carrick beside the command chair. 'Do you reckon we're on a fishery cruiser or is this really the royal yacht in disguise?'

'If I see a woman wandering around wearing a crown I'll let you know,' said Carrick dryly. 'What's your problem?'

Ferguson glanced round at the helmsman and lowered his voice. 'Our captain. I thought we were only going to ferry ballot boxes this trip –'

'Right,' agreed Carrick.

'Well, while you were in dreamland he announced a surprise ship's inspection,' declared Ferguson flatly. 'It's going on now – he's checking everywhere, with Jumbo Wills trotting at his heels.'

'Hard luck, Jumbo,' mused Carrick. 'So?'

'So why?' persisted Ferguson. 'I heard him. "Clean this, paint that – and every second thing is a damned disgrace!" ' He made it a passable copy of Shannon's snarl, then puzzled. 'You're chief officer. Could there be something else going on we don't know about?'

'This trip?' Carrick shook his head. 'No, politicians just worry him.'

'They worry everybody,' said Ferguson, still suspicious. 'We'll berth at Feanport in another couple of hours. Maybe we'll know then.'

Leaving him still muttering, Carrick left the bridge and headed aft. Keeping to the open deck as the best way to avoid Shannon's inspection tour, he paused and narrowed his eyes against the sunlight. An old black-funnelled inter-island cargo ship was passing them to starboard, making her slow way south. She had cattle penned on her open foredeck and he could even hear their faint bellowing across the water as if the luckless animals knew their next stop would be a mainland market.

A different kind of bellowing was coming from the scuba compartment near the stern. Petty Officer Clapper Bell was singing. The door lay open and as Carrick entered the big Glasgow-Irish bo'sun broke off and beamed a greeting.

'Safe enough in here, sir,' said Bell with a wink. 'The Old Man's been an' gone.'

'Good.' Carrick sat on a crate of diving spares while Bell finished an adjustment he was making to one of their aqualung harnesses. 'How was it?'

'The usual – you filthy sailor, get the place cleaned up. An' our Mr Wills lookin' like he'd already received the full wrath o' God, marked "Personal".' Bell set the harness aside, straddled another crate, and produced his cigarettes. 'Smoke?'

'You filthy sailor, it's a filthy habit,' said Carrick sourly.

'Stopped again?' Bell made a deliberate performance of lighting a cigarette for himself and sucked the smoke happily. 'Eh . . . how about a wee side bet on it, like the last time?'

'No way,' said Carrick grimly.

'Feelin' touchy already?' Bell enjoyed himself. 'A pity. I could have used the money, after a week's leave an' that –'

'I'll believe it,' agreed Carrick.

Clapper Bell's leave usually revolved around some mammoth poker game. He grinned a little. His own seven days had ended up differently this time. Conscience had sent him visiting his parents, who ran a small farm. He'd ended up mending fences and working harder than he ever did aboard *Marlin*.

'I remember the last time we were at Feanport,' said Bell suddenly. 'The locals were havin' a little war all their own wi' some Norwegian shark-boats. Three years ago, that was – right before you joined us.' He considered the racks of scuba gear around the small compartment. 'We should be comin' into the Brannan Sound about now, the approach channel. You know, if we've a chance, there's one or two good wrecks worth a dive around here.'

'Maybe.' Carrick was doubtful. 'It depends on a few things, Clapper – like those ballot boxes.'

'Stuff them,' grumbled Bell. 'I'll tell you who'll win any kind of election up here – the first idiot who promises to cut taxes more than anyone else.'

Carrick grinned. The previous Member of Parliament for the Lochard constituency had been a tearaway Scottish Nationalist who had held the seat by a knife-edge majority. His death in a car crash had put four candidates in the ring and they were all making promises. But even the press and

TV pundits were refusing to guess which way the votes would go.

He glanced around the scuba compartment for a moment, his sympathies with Bell. They hadn't had much diving practice on the last couple of patrols and that was never a good situation. Then another thought struck him.

'The last time you were up this way, did you come across an old hag called the Witch of the Isles?'

'Aye, we did.' Bell drew irritatingly on his cigarette. 'Uh – who told you about her?'

'Shannon.'

'Did he give her a name?' queried Bell.

Carrick shook his head.

'Her married name's Vullan – Dorothy Vullan,' said Bell with a soft chuckle. 'She's not young, but she's no old hag. She's a rich witch too. That village cop MacKenzie I told you about says she owns a dam' great chunk of Feanport.'

'And a golden broomstick too?' Carrick raised a caustic eyebrow. 'What's the witch bit all about, Clapper?'

'It just runs in the family,' shrugged Bell. 'They drowned one o' her ancestors for puttin' the hex on a local preacher an' her family's been stuck with the reputation ever since.' He paused and winked. 'They've found it useful. Even today the Feanport locals avoid a quarrel wi' the Witch o' the Isles – just in case things start goin' wrong around them.'

Carrick wasn't particularly surprised. People in the islands were hard-headed, intelligent and had their deep freezes and TV sets like anyone else. But deep down they still had the tendril remnants of an older way of life – remnants that came to the surface from time to time in the most surprising ways.

'Look, I still think we should talk about those wrecks,' declared Bell earnestly. 'I've got them marked an' if you've got a bit o' time to spare –'

'Show me,' invited Carrick.

Beaming, the bo'sun produced a creased, much-stained Admiralty chart, unfolded it, and began explaining.

Half an hour later they'd more or less agreed that the best of the selection of sunken shipping available on Clapper Bell's chart was probably an old destroyer which had been wrecked in World War One and was supposed to be lying in about forty fathoms of water close to the reef which had finished her. But as Bell made enthusiastic noises about what was involved he stopped suddenly and gave a surprised glance at Carrick.

There had been a change in the note from *Marlin*'s diesels. A moment passed then a new shudder ran through her hull, her engine revolutions began climbing and her deck began to heel. The fishery cruiser was going somewhere new, and in a hurry.

They reached the door of the scuba compartment together and Bell gave an interested grunt. The creaming white wash now building from *Marlin*'s stern showed they were curving away from the shoreline.

'Trouble?' asked Bell hopefully.

'Could be,' said Carrick as the thunder of air being sucked down to feed the diesels kept increasing. 'I'll let you know.'

He hurried along the deck, grabbing a rail for a handhold as spray drenched aboard, silver in the bright sunlight. All the signs were that Bell was right. Some seamen were readying one of *Marlin*'s boats, extra lookouts were in position on the bridge wings, and the shuddering note of power underfoot was still growing. As Carrick reached the foot of the companionway steps leading to the bridge Ferguson came galloping down and shoved past him, heading aft.

Carrick went on up. He found Captain Shannon already in the command chair with Jumbo Wills in position beside the bridge intercom and a petty officer standing by the helmsman. Shannon rasped an order and a moment later a signal rocket soared up, to burst high and white.

'Dead ahead, mister,' said Shannon briefly, greeting him with a nod. 'Three miles, maybe. See for yourself.'

Carrick took the bridge glasses from the bearded, moon-faced figure and deftly adjusted the focus a fraction. Shannon's eyes weren't as good as they'd been a few years back. Then, as he stared through them, his lips puckered in a silent whistle of understanding.

A thin pillar of smoke showed ahead, rising from a fishing boat which lay beam-on to the waves, rolling sluggishly and low in the water. As Carrick kept the glasses trained, *Marlin* vibrating on, he saw the tiny yellow blob of a liferaft tossing in the sea beside the helpless craft and the way her wheelhouse was a broken mess.

'She's drifting west,' said Shannon curtly. 'Better look there too.'

Carrick did, and understood. A long, white line of broken water lay waiting there, an occasional black fang of rock showing then disappearing again.

'Any radio contact, sir?' he asked, lowering the powerful glasses.

'We can't raise her,' frowned Shannon. 'Ferguson saw her first, on radar, and wondered what the hell she was doing so close to those rocks. Then she fired two distress flares and we spotted the smoke.' He swung round in the command chair. 'Mr Wills –'

'Sir?' Jumbo Wills practically sprang to his side.

'Don't damned well do that,' snarled Shannon indignantly. 'You make me nervous. Pass the word I want a tow-line readied. Then let them have another rocket – they can probably use the encouragement.' He faced Carrick again while Wills turned to the intercom phone. 'As soon as we've closed, take a boat over to her mister, Do what you can to help. But her people come first. If she's sinking – I want no fancy risks. Understood?'

Carrick nodded, looking out again to where the thin plume of smoke was now visible to the naked eye. Even at full power, it was going to take *Marlin* another seven or eight minutes to get within hailing distance of the crippled fishing boat. Presuming she stayed afloat that long.

The signal rocket Shannon had ordered roared up from *Marlin* a moment later and burst high in the clear blue sky. Carrick said nothing, but he had an idea that for once he and Shannon were probably sharing the same puzzled thought.

The weather was good and the sea was calm. Exactly how and when had the boat ahead got herself into this kind of trouble – and why?

Ten minutes later *Marlin*'s launch nosed in to touch the wallowing hull of the drifting fishing boat. As the two craft grated, Webb Carrick made a scrambling jump across – and a big, bearded fisherman waiting on the fishing boat's foam-washed deck grabbed his arm and hauled him firmly aboard.

'Never thought I'd be glad to see a Fishery man,' said the fisherman hoarsely. His face, beak-nosed and weathered like granite, twisted a weary grin. 'But I'd welcome the devil himself right now.'

Carrick nodded, eased the small two-way radio he had on a sling over one shoulder, and glanced round. The launch was already edging clear again, waiting for orders, with Clapper Bell and three of *Marlin*'s hands aboard. A cable's distance out, almost as near as Shannon dare because of outlying rocks, the fishery cruiser lay with her diesels cut back to a slow, pulsing exhaust.

'Any injured aboard?' he asked as a first priority.

'One man – not too badly,' said the bearded man and gave a grim shrug. 'We're the *Rachel*, out of Feanport. I'm Angus Grant, skipper and owner, for what that's worth now.'

The hull gave a sullen roll in the swell and fresh foam lapped across the wet decking, emphasizing how low in the water the *Rachel* was lying.

'Better show me how things are,' said Carrick, knowing he had decisions ahead and little time in which to make them.

'Come to the wheelhouse,' said Grant shortly. 'The others are there anyway.'

They went across the deck to the shattered wheel-house where the other four members of the *Rachel*'s crew were waiting. Two were fishing hands, both in their early thirties, and they greeted Carrick with relieved grins as they stood back to let him enter. Another man about the same age lay inside, propped against what had been a doorway, wrapped in an old blanket. Most of the hair had been scorched from his head and he was moaning a little, his eyes half-closed.

But the remaining member of the *Rachel*'s crew was a small, slim girl with long chestnut hair which was soaked and bedraggled. Kneeling beside the injured man, holding a flask of water to his lips, she looked round at Carrick with calm grey eyes and a serious face. She wore a blue jersey, slacks and seaboots like the others.

'My daughter Shona,' said Grant, then shrugged ruefully. 'She came out with us for a pleasure trip.'

Carrick bent over the injured man, then glanced at the girl.

'How is he?' he asked.

'Lucky,' she said quietly. 'Burns and shock, maybe a fractured rib – but that's all. He could have been killed.'

'Aye, he was lucky,' said Grant heavily, then, as Carrick

rose, he took a glance at the others as if for support before he went on. 'Things are maybe the same way with the *Rachel* . . . not as bad as they look, mister. She isn't sinking and we've been riding like this for a good while now. Maybe if your ship got a line aboard us and we tried a tow –'

He stopped there, eyeing Carrick, waiting.

Squeezing past, Carrick crossed to the little companionway hatch at the front of the wheelhouse and peered down into the dark interior of what had been a cabin below. Almost all he could see was a swirl of water topped by a scum of debris.

'It's worth trying,' persisted Grant.

Still Carrick didn't answer. He left the hatchway, went to the wheelhouse door, and frowned out at the broken line of water to starboard which marked the fangs of the main reef. The distance between the *Rachel* and those hungry rocks was still shrinking as the boat drifted with the current.

But it might still be worth a try, as Grant claimed. The *Rachel* was a standard sixty-foot motor fishing vessel with a wooden hull, a kind that possessed plenty of built-in buoyancy. Damage on her deck area seemed restricted to the wheelhouse and the smoke seen by *Marlin*'s lookouts was explained by the few last wisps still rising from a smouldering pile of nets on the for'ard fish hatch cover.

'We used the last two flares when we saw you,' said Shona Grant, as if reading his mind. 'Then we grabbed anything left that might burn to make a smoke signal.'

Carrick nodded and turned to Grant. 'Skipper, what's your damage below?'

'We're holed badly on the waterline, starboard side.' Grant's bearded, beak-nosed face tightened at the thought. 'A gas cylinder blew up in the galley, like a dam' bomb going off, and punched straight through the hull. The wheelhouse took the rest o' the blast through the hatch and our radio was wrecked like everything else.'

'And what happened to him?' asked Carrick, pointing to the injured man.

'He was in the galley when it happened. I'd sent him down to light the gas stove an' brew some tea.' Grant shook his head in bewilderment. 'Don't ask me why he wasn't killed down there. His brother was in the wheelhouse and got blown out through the door.'

'His brother?' Carrick glanced at the two fishing hands.

'That's me.' It was the taller of the two, lanky, with long, dark hair, who spoke. He had a gash on his forehead. 'I'm Donnie MacLean and that's my brother Willie over there. Och, but he'll be fine' – he gave a deliberate wink towards the injured man, who managed to shape a faint, painful grin – 'an' that blowtorch hair-style suits him, eh?' Hardly pausing, he gestured at his companion. 'This is our cousin Lachie MacLean.'

'Cousin Willie will be fine,' agreed Lachie MacLean, a chunky fair-haired individual with a wispy straggle of moustache. He nodded seriously. 'It takes more than a wee accident to kill a MacLean.'

'Shut up, both of you,' said Grant despairingly. He turned impatiently to Carrick and chewed hard on his lip for a moment. 'It's up to you. Will you ask your captain to try a tow?'

For a long moment the steady wash of the sea and the throb of the idling launch, back alongside again, were the only sounds. They all watched him, even the injured Willie MacLean. Carrick glanced at Shona Grant, saw the silent pleading in her grey eyes, but still made up his mind in terms of a practical gamble.

'I'll suggest it,' he agreed in a flat voice.

'Good.' It came like a sigh of relief from Grant, then a sudden caution showed on the bearded skipper's face. 'Mind you, it's only a tow I'm wanting. My crew stay aboard –'

'We're not hunting salvage money, skipper,' said Carrick patiently. 'But we'll move Willie – and your daughter better go with him. She can give Captain Shannon the story.'

Grant relaxed and nodded. Bringing the little walkie-talkie to his lips, Carrick thumbed the transmitter button and called *Marlin*. Shannon's voice answered immediately.

'You've taken long enough, mister,' came his crackling comment. 'Well, report.'

'She's the *Rachel* out of Feanport, badly holed and one crewman injured,' replied Carrick, unruffled. 'The skipper wants to try a tow.'

There was a pause, a burst of louder static, then a grunt. 'What's your opinion, mister?'

'That we haven't much time,' said Carrick flatly.

'Understood.' Shannon's manner was suddenly and totally professional. 'Let's get started, mister. I'll try and shade nearer to you. But it's your feet that get wet if you're wrong.'

Grinning, Carrick lowered the walkie-talkie and beckoned the launch in. She came alongside in seconds, rubbing the *Rachel*'s old motor-tyre fenders, being held against them as Clapper Bell fed quick, short bursts of power to the engine. Two of her crew scrambled aboard the fishing boat and helped move Willie MacLean as gently as possible from one craft to the other.

While that was happening, Carrick took the chance to give Clapper Bell a quick rundown on the situation and what they'd need. Then, seeing MacLean settled in the launch, he looked round for Shona Grant just as she came over from the wheelhouse.

'Ready?' Carrick looked at her and marvelled. Somehow, she'd found a moment to comb her wet, straggling hair into order.

'Yes.' She stopped beside him. 'My father – he's stubborn, like a mule. But he loves this boat, so –'

'We'll cope with him,' promised Carrick.

Clapper Bell edged the launch closer again. Shona Grant swung down into it, settled at the stern thwarts, and the little craft moved away in a haze of blue exhaust.

CHAPTER TWO

It remained a close-run race against the current and the reef. Passing the tow-line across to the fishing boat and securing it was a struggle on its own, and Shannon sent extra help to assist, headed by Ferguson. Then Clapper Bell returned while that was still in progress and dragged a load of big plastic flotation bags aboard the *Rachel.*

Carrick left Ferguson to worry about the tow-line and joined Bell. With Angus Grant assisting from the deck the two men plunged into the cold, water-filled darkness of the fishing boat's hull and began the laborious task of placing the flotation bags and triggering the CO2 cartridges which inflated them.

Each bag meant extra buoyancy, slightly better odds for later. But it was a dirty, dangerous business of wading chest-high, sometimes ducking totally under, regularly colliding with unseen obstacles and bobbing fitments. There was even the hazard of getting clear as each flotation bag mushroomed out. Their fingers numbed, their feet soon had lost all feeling.

They were in the cramped space of the engine-room, struggling to jam an inflated bag under a metal beam, when the whole hull suddenly shuddered and rolled. Thrown off his feet, banging his head on something hard as he went down, Carrick came up spluttering. Clapper Bell had gone under too and surfaced cursing – then as the hull's shudder changed and the roll became a slow pitch they splashed and clawed their way back to the deck.

Then Clapper Bell's cursing changed to a bellow of delight. The *Rachel* was moving, the tow-line connecting her to *Marlin* already stretched taut and water pouring from its length. Gradually, still lurching and quivering, the fishing boat came round as the long grey shape of the fishery cruiser kept up the delicate manoeuvre.

Together, they stumbled over to the wheelhouse where Ferguson was standing with Angus Grant beside him. A little way aft, the two MacLeans and the little group of *Marlin*'s hands were standing grinning.

'Finished down there?' asked Ferguson politely. Then

the grey-haired junior second's habitually sour expression thawed and he thumbed towards the stern. 'There's your safety margin.'

Carrick winced. While he'd been below they'd drifted until the line of the reef was only about a boat-length away. Dark, individual fangs of rock were clearly visible among the white of the breaking swell.

The radio in Ferguson's hand crackled. He murmured an answer into it and a moment later *Marlin*'s siren bellowed. As the throb of her diesels began to deepen the black diamond towing signal rose to her masthead. Then the tow-line creaked to a new strain and the fishing boat began moving ahead, slowly at first then the crawl gradually increasing as she was hauled away from what should have been her grave.

'I owe a debt to all your people,' said Angus Grant huskily. 'I –'

'Skipper, I'd keep my thanks till you're back in Feanport,' said Ferguson dryly, cutting him short. He saw Carrick's raised eyebrow and nodded. 'Captain Shannon reckons on a three-hour haul, but it's still the nearest harbour.'

'Aye,' said Grant grimly. 'And once I get back, once I've seen this boat safe on a slipway and Willie MacLean on his way to hospital, I've a few things to sort out.' He stopped there, his face granite-hard for a moment, then cleared his throat heavily and produced a flask from his pocket. 'Carrick, you and the bo'sun look like you could both use a dram. Medicinal, I'd call it.'

Bell took first gulp from the flask. Then it was Carrick's turn and once he'd felt the raw spirit burn its way down he glanced at Bell and grinned. Their faces were streaked with oil, water was dribbling from their sodden clothing, and they looked more like rescued than rescuers. He took another swallow from the flask, then passed it back to Bell.

The men aft hauled the yellow rubber liferaft back aboard, working with a new relaxed air. The mood was infectious – the little fishing boat was wallowing along at a steady three knots, her bow meeting the low green swell in a steady, chunking rhythm as she followed *Marlin*'s wake.

'This captain of yours,' said Angus Grant in a slightly worried voice. He paused, frowning, and rubbed a hand across his beard. 'How much does he know about towing? There's some advice I'd maybe give him –'

Carrick kept a stony face at the thought, but Ferguson

who had been listening to a new message coming over the radio, saved him from having to reply.

'Your boat, our tow, skipper,' he said crisply. 'I'd forget about the advice, but Captain Shannon does want to talk with you.' He glanced at Carrick and nodded. 'You and Bell are ordered back – and you've to bring Skipper Grant.'

'Leave the *Rachel* – now?' Grant hesitated.

'The MacLeans are here, so you've a crew aboard,' reminded Carrick, guessing Grant was thinking of salvage law again. 'You'd better come. Anyway, meeting Captain Shannon is an experience.'

'People say that about bein' hit by a truck,' muttered Clapper Bell, and ignored the glare it brought from Ferguson.

They made the transfer by *Marlin*'s launch a few minutes later, scrambled from there up a ladder to the fishery cruiser's main deck, and discovered Captain James Shannon had come down from the bridge to meet them. He had Shona Grant with him and her father hugged her for a moment.

'Ah – welcome aboard, skipper,' said Shannon, shaking hands with Grant. He gave a faint smile at the way Grant kept one arm round his daughter. 'I've already got to know the other half of your partnership.'

The two bearded men, Shannon small and plump, Grant large and raw-boned, faced each other for a moment and then Grant nodded.

'I'm in your debt, Captain Shannon,' he said with a dignified formality, then glanced at Shona. 'How's Willie MacLean?'

'Resting now, in the sickbay,' she assured him. Snug in a borrowed change of clothing topped by one of Shannon's duffel coats, she smiled at her father while her long chestnut hair was teased by the breeze. 'They've radioed to Feanport for an ambulance to meet us.'

'Now I want to know what happened, your version, skipper,' said Shannon briskly. 'We'll talk in my day-cabin.' He paused, switched his attention to Carrick, and made an odd noise deep in his throat. 'Mister, you and the bo'sun both look like you fell off a garbage scow. Do something about it.'

Then he turned on his heel, leading Grant and the girl away. A deckhand standing near chuckled, then quickly froze any expression from his face as Clapper Bell glared at him.

'Easy, Clapper,' murmured Carrick. 'That's his idea of a compliment. You know how he works – never give a pat on the back if you can manage a kick up the tail.'

'An' he's good at it,' admitted Bell wryly. 'None better.'

They parted, and Carrick went down to his cabin. It was another half-hour before he came back on deck, having managed to scrub clean, change into dry clothes, and snatch something to eat in the wardroom.

Pausing beside a deckhouse, he looked aft. The *Rachel* was still riding along steadily at the end of her tow-line and he reckoned *Marlin* was now nursing the disabled fishing boat along at about five knots through the continued light swell.

'Aye, she's taking it well,' said Angus Grant, surprising him by emerging from the lee of the deckhouse. The bearded fisherman gave a slightly sheepish grimace. 'I came along here to hide from your Captain Shannon. That man asks more questions than an Admiralty Board.'

Carrick nodded and leaned his hands on the rail. The mainland was about four miles to starboard, a jutting headland of rock topped by the slim white pillar of a lighthouse. To port and slightly astern a low black patch of rock broke the water about a mile away.

'Another ten miles, no more, and we're at Feanport,' declared Grant, joining him. 'We're well into the Brannan Sound now – we call that headland Broch Point.' A bleaker note entered his voice. 'There's a name for that patch of rock to port. We call it the Witchrock around here.'

'The Witchrock.' Carrick's interest stirred a little. 'I've heard that Feanport has its own resident witch.'

'Aye.' Grant's hands tightened on the rail. 'And the first damned witch in that family gave the Witchrock its name six or so generations back – she was marooned out there to drown.' He snorted hard. 'Some of the old ideas were good ones.'

'Meaning you've a problem with the present generation?' queried Carrick.

'I never said that.' Grant's eyes were still on the wet black hump of rock. 'But I'll give you one piece of advice, Carrick. While you're in Feanport, treat the Brannan Sound and all it contains with care – so-called witches included.'

'I'll do that.' Carrick knew better than to smile. 'How about your own troubles, skipper? Does Willie MacLean have any idea why that gas cylinder exploded?'

'He's in no state to talk about it,' said Grant curtly. His mouth shaped a sudden, tight line. 'And I'm tired of answering questions. I told Shannon that before I left him – do I have to say the same to you?'

Then, before Carrick could answer, the fisherman had spun on his heel and was striding off along the deck. Carrick stared after him till he'd gone through a companionway door. Whatever was wrong, he'd somehow scraped a ragged nerve-ending as far as Angus Grant was concerned.

Deciding that finding out more would have to wait, he headed for the bridge. Jumbo Wills had the watch with the duty helmsman and a leading seaman was keeping a permanent eye on their tow. When Carrick arrived, Wills was lounging in the command chair with his hands clasped behind his head.

'Good afternoon, Admiral,' said Carrick stonily. 'Sorry to disturb you.'

Wills jerked in surprise then grinned and climbed down from the chair.

'The gentleman from the garbage scow,' he retorted. 'You came at a good time. Out to starboard, Webb – what do you make of these two?'

Carrick looked and then reached for the bridge glasses. Two big, dark-hulled Norwegian shark-boats swam into focus through the lenses. They were pairing their way down the Brannan Sound from the north, heading for some new catching ground. And like Wills, he knew them instantly – on *Marlin*'s last patrol she had caught both boats hunting inside the limits.

'Log the sighting, Jumbo,' he ordered, lowering the bridge glasses. 'Leave it at that.'

Wills nodded. Gradually the two Norwegian boats came closer, obviously curious about the black diamond towing signal at the fishery cruiser's masthead. Men appeared on the deck of both shark-boats, staring, then a signal lamp blinked a greeting from the leading boat's wheelhouse.

'Answer it?' queried Willis.

'Thank them,' said Carrick shortly, knowing the greeting was genuine. There were no nationality barriers among the fishing fleets when it came to a man against the sea situation.

Wills took a signal lamp out on the bridge wing, triggered a reply in his ragged Morse, then returned. As the shark-boats headed away, swinging back on their original course, he eyed Carrick cautiously.

'Webb, you know the Old Man didn't get to finish ship's rounds because of the *Rachel* panic,' He paused, saw Carrick's expression, and nodded. 'That's right, he wants you to finish it. He's in the radio room if you want to check –'

Carrick shook his head, took the clipboard hanging from a hook below the bridge intercom, and scanned the scribbled notes. He'd been left with the lower deck and engine-room.

Completing what remained of Shannon's inspection tour took about an hour. It was dull, it was routine and it was necessary – but at the end of it the lower-deck problems came down to little more than a jammed sea-water intake while for once Andy Shaw, as chief engineer, could produce only one item that mattered. He had a worry about *Marlin*'s main generator, suspected a bearing, and wanted Shannon to know he intended tackling the job as soon as they were berthed in Feanport.

Finished at that, Carrick climbed his way back up to the bridge – then stopped as he reached it and swore under his breath. One or two things seemed to have changed while he'd been below.

For a starting surprise, Shona Grant was at the helm, her hands resting lightly on the polished wheel-spokes, while Jumbo Wills more or less breathed down her neck. *Marlin* was nosing her way up a mile-wide channel between the mainland and a collection of low, barren islands and weed-covered rocks.

'Signed on an extra hand?' he asked mildly, going past them and returning the clipboard to its hook.

'Uh – Shona was keen to have a look around,' said Wills hastily. He grinned uneasily at the regular helmsman, who was watching from one side with a wary, not totally happy expression. 'Right, Tam, back to work.'

Shona Grant let the helmsman take over again, a slight twinkle in her grey eyes.

'No need to worry, Chief Officer,' she said calmly. 'My father had me steering a fishing boat before I started school – standing on an orange box to reach the controls.'

'You're promoted to navigator.' Carrick's gaze strayed

briefly towards the coastline. 'And you're not far from home now.'

'Another couple of miles to go, round the next headland. It's a deep water approach with a marked channel.' Her eyes strayed round the bridge with a genuine interest. 'I like your *Marlin*.'

'Captain Shannon's *Marlin*,' corrected Carrick dryly. He turned to Wills. 'Where is he, anyway?'

'Talking to Angus Grant again – but he says everything is arranged for us at Feanport.' Wills thumbed towards the empty command chair. 'Give him another few minutes and he'll be back. Ever known the Old Man let anyone else take us into port when there's an audience?'

'This time he's welcome to it,' said Carrick patiently. 'Start checking our readiness status. Get Clapper Bell to muster some extra hands aft, call Ferguson and make sure everything's happy on the *Rachel*. You know the rest of it.'

Shrugging, Jumbo Wills crossed to the intercom, lifted the handset, and went to work. While the freckle-faced second mate punched buttons and talked, Shona Grant moved over towards the port bridge wing and looked over towards the dark line of little islands.

Carrick studied her. Slim, a fraction under medium height, certainly in her mid-twenties, she was the kind of girl whom men usually called attractive rather than pretty – and tended to remember. The long chestnut hair framed a delicately boned, lightly tanned face which had a slightly snubbed nose, and like most girls from the lonely north-west coast every movement she made held a supple, natural grace.

Shona Grant turned, beckoned him nearer, and pointed to a dilapidated old boat which was coming into sight, moored in the lee of the nearest islet.

'There's your welcome to Feanport,' she said with a wry humour. 'We haven't much in the way of tourist attractions. That's the *Piddock*, out gathering seaweed. She feeds a processing plant north of the harbour.'

An old, converted herring drifter, brown paint badly weathered and faded, most of the *Piddock*'s deckworks had been removed. In their place she had a bucket-grab installed near the bow. As they watched, a low rumble came across the water and the long-toothed grab swung out, to plunge into the sea. In a few moments the workboat's winch gear rumbled again and the grab was hauled up, a mass of dripping wrack and kelp weed clutched between its teeth.

'Local enterprise or outsiders?' asked Carrick, curious.

'Local, strictly Feanport.' Shona Grant waited while the grab swung in and two men with rakes appeared on the *Piddock*'s deck, guiding their catch into her hold. 'Or the Vullan family, which is pretty much the same thing. Have you heard about them?'

'I've been told they have a share in most things here.' He kept his eyes on the workboat. Seaweed was an old island harvest, one which had been almost abandoned for a time but now mattered again. Modern industry had new techniques for using the weed in everything from chemical manufacture to food production. 'And about the Witch of the Isles – she sounds formidable.'

'I happen to like her, like her a lot,' said Shona Grant firmly. 'I won't pretend everybody does – Dorothy Vullan just happens to be that kind of person.'

'Who runs the weed operation?' asked Carrick.

'Her husband, Milne Vullan – at least he started it, then brought in a man called John Marsh to manage things.' She hesitated slightly, then added, 'Marsh isn't local, but he does a reasonable enough job.'

The fishery cruiser and her tow began to leave the old workboat astern. Carrick stayed silent for a moment, faintly puzzled.

'You say you like Dorothy Vullan. When I talked to your father, he made it plain he felt differently about her,' he said frankly. 'Why?'

'It's a quarrel that goes a long way back – I told you he was mule-tempered at times.' Shona Grant gave a rueful grimace. 'Right now, he's in a new rage about her but he just won't talk to me about it. All I've got out of him is a mutter that he won't let any damned woman, witch or bitch, give him orders.'

A grunted plea for attention from the helmsman brought Carrick round. The man eased the wheel's spokes a fraction and nodded ahead. The fishery cruiser was approaching a low, heather-covered headland and behind it a large bay was opening up.

'That's Feanport,' agreed Shona Grant. She flicked a loose strand of hair back from her forehead and rested a hand for a moment on the bridge rail. 'I'd better go and find my father – and look in on Willie MacLean, make sure they've got him ready to move.'

Behind them, Jumbo Wills finished hastily on the intercom, hung up, and came over.

'We'll see you ashore later, won't we?' he asked hopefully.

'In a place the size of Feanport you don't see people, you trip over them,' she said cheerfully, and left them.

Jumbo Wills waited till she'd gone then gave a long, sad sigh.

'What's wrong with me?' he asked plaintively. 'The only people I ever got to save from a watery grave were a bunch of hairy fishermen.'

The helmsman treated them both to a gap-toothed grin, a souvenir of a boarding party *Marlin* had once put aboard a Polish trawler off Barra Head. Then he looked past them, switched to a quick, warning frown, and turned his full attention to *Marlin*'s heading as Captain Shannon erupted from the direction of the chartroom like a menacing nautical gnome.

'Am I interrupting anything?' he asked Carrick acidly, totally ignoring Wills.

'No, sir.' Carrick met the glare with a wooden calm which he knew annoyed Shannon more than anything short of mutiny. 'We're at full readiness to enter harbour – tow included.'

'Then let's get on with it.' Shannon took another scowl around then hauled himself up into the command chair. 'Till it's done, keep that damned skipper of the *Rachel* away from me. He's as close-mouthed and stubborn as – as –'

'As a mule?' suggested Carrick.

'Yes.' Shannon's mouth tightened and for a moment the scowl gave way to a more pensive look. 'But he could be a worried mule, an angry mule – or both. I'm going to find out why, because I've a feeling it could matter.'

Fean Bay, a bite out of the land almost two miles wide and about a mile deep, was a place where the sea met a series of sheer rock faces backed by hills. But from the moment *Marlin* rounded the headland the bay's benefits as a natural anchorage were immediately obvious. Feanport itself, a straggle of a village with a big stone breakwater enclosing the harbour, lay at the head of the bay – and about half a mile out from the shore a long, narrow island, low and a fertile shade of green, offered the fishing village an additional, natural shelter from the open sea.

An escort was waiting. Two broad-beamed fishing boats, idling close beside the island, moved out and took up station astern as the fishery cruiser and her tow crept on. Their skippers talked briefly by radio to Captain Shannon then kept their boats in the same positions, professionals who knew what they had to do and how to do it.

The little convoy slowly passed the long island. People lived there. Carrick saw a scatter of small buildings, then a large white house close by the shore with steps leading down to a small pier. A dark blue launch, big and with the lines of a one-time naval boat, had just left the pier and was heading for Feanport. But she gave the convoy a wide berth and vanished inside the harbour.

Marlin stopped engines about five hundred yards from the outer breakwater. As she rode gently in the slight swell, the tow-line sagging, a boat was lowered and took Angus Grant back to the *Rachel*. When it returned, it brought Ferguson and fishery cruiser men who had been with him. At the same time, Angus Grant cast off his end of the tow-line.

The fishermen were on their own. Smoothly and neatly the two Feanport boats came in on either side of the *Rachel* and in moments she was cradled between them, secured tightly fore and aft.

The black towing diamond had come down from *Marlin*'s foremast. A klaxon horn sounded from one of the Feanport boats then, their propellers churning busily, nursing the damaged *Rachel* between them, they headed in through the breakwater entrance.

'One worry less.' Captain Shannon delivered his verdict with a degree of relief from the bridge wing, where he'd watched the operation. He turned, beckoned Carrick over, then glanced past him at Jumbo Wills. 'We'll lie here till the harbour tower signals they're clear. Stretcher party ready to take that fishing hand ashore?'

'Ready sir,' agreed Wills. 'Skipper Grant's daughter is with him too.'

'Right.' Shannon looked out across the water at the island, then switched his attention to Carrick. 'That's Fean Island over there – deep water on three sides, but all rock and foul ground to the north. Don't try to take anything bigger than a rowing boat out that way.' He paused and scratched at his beard. 'The big house on the island is Fean House, Dorothy Vullan's family home. I've more than a notion she'll be inviting some of us over – it's almost a tradition when a fishery cruiser comes to Feanport.'

'I hope she does,' said Carrick evenly. 'I talked to Angus Grant, like you did.'

Shannon stiffened, faced Carrick for a moment in silence, then nodded. He said softly, 'The chartroom, mister. Not here.'

Carrick followed him across the bridge, conscious of Jumbo Wills' curious glance, and into the little chartroom. Shannon heeled the door shut behind him.

'How much did you get out of Grant?' he demanded.

'Next to nothing,' admitted Carrick. 'It was what he wouldn't say that mattered.'

Shannon sighed, leaned his hands on the chartroom table, and scowled at the scarred surface of the food.

'That makes two of us.' He paused, as if still trying to make up his mind. 'I met him briefly, last time I was here – he's a widower, and the girl is all the family he has. She doesn't live in Feanport now, she's just home for a couple of weeks' leave.'

'Sir?' Carrick raised a surprised eyebrow.

'That's one thing he will talk about,' agreed Shannon. 'Grant's proud as hell about her. His Shona seems to have brains as well as looks.' He sniffed, making it doubtful whether he totally approved. 'She works for one of the North Sea oil outfits, Anglo-Norge, on the research side. Probably earns twice what you do.'

'That wouldn't be hard,' said Carrick dryly.

Shannon grunted and made a show of tidying away a couple of charts. Carrick waited, the deck vibrating gently underfoot as the twin diesels idled. Through the chartroom window he could see a solitary gull had perched on the starboard searchlight mounting. Other gulls, at least a score, were circling and crying overhead while they probably wondered about this new arrival and what kind of food it might provide.

'Do something for me, mister,' said Shannon suddenly. 'Once we've berthed, explore your way around that harbour. Sniff the air, get the atmosphere of the place. I've got a feeling I don't like, a feeling there's something wrong.'

'Involving Grant, sir?'

Shannon shrugged. 'Maybe, maybe more than that – I don't know.' He took a pack of cigarettes from his pocket, stuck one in his mouth, and lit it with a battered gun-metal lighter. He took a long draw of the smoke, let it filter out again through his beard, then asked, 'Notice anything unusual about the two Feanport boats who collected the *Rachel*?'

'No.' Carrick stared at him, puzzled.

'Each of them had a rowan-tree branch tied to the foremast with red cord. Rowan and red cord – that's the old island way of fending off witchcraft.'

'In case helping Angus Grant got them on a witchcraft black list?' Carrick couldn't hide his sheer disbelief. 'Hell, we're talking about people who have TV sets and deep freezes, sir. They send their kids to college, they're clever enough to make monkeys out of the Inland Revenue, they –'

'If they're worried, what's wrong with a little old-fashioned insurance?' interrupted Shannon testily. 'And if they're worried, what's going on? Dorothy Vullan always made a joke of this Witch of the Isles business.' He tapped the chart table with his stubby fingertips. 'I don't think the girl knows anything, and it's probably the same with his crew. Grant won't talk – but see him, tell him we want to inspect what's left of the gas cylinder that exploded. Keep it casual, make some kind of a noise about a routine report. Understood?'

Carrick nodded. Over on the breakwater wall a signal lamp had begun winking in their direction. Shannon had seen it too, the all-clear signal. He grunted and drew on his cigarette again before mashing it out in an ashtray.

'One last thing,' he said bleakly. 'I got it from the girl, when we were down in sickbay seeing how that injured fishing hand was making out. The Feanport constable, a man named MacKenzie, got himself drowned about ten days ago – he went fishing one night and his body was washed up three days later. When I talked to Grant, he didn't even mention it.' He paused. 'I'm not saying there has to be any connection, mister.'

'No,' agreed Carrick softly. 'But Clapper Bell will want to know. MacKenzie was a friend of his.'

'I'll tell him.' Shannon nodded unemotionally. 'All right, I've a ship to berth. Let's do it sweetly – whether you see them or not, we're going to have plenty of spectators.'

Ten minutes later, after an impeccable piece of ship-handling on Shannon's part, *Marlin* tied up at a vacant berth on the south quay of Feanport harbour. Her nearest neighbour was a coaster unloading cement, beyond that was a small oil tanker which was getting ready to sail, and the rest of the harbour was a clutter of fishing boats of every shape and size. Most were Feanport's boats by their registration letters, all had landed their day's catch, and the usual bustle of buyers were moving from one small mountain of overflowing fish boxes to the next.

An ambulance threaded its way through the confusion and reached *Marlin* almost at the same time as her gangway was run out. Another moment then, as the ambulance doors opened, Willie MacLean was carried down the gangway on a stretcher. Shona Grant was with him, waited until MacLean had been put aboard the ambulance, and stayed for a moment to thank the stretcher party once the vehicle had driven off again.

Carrick came back from checking the bow mooring lines in time to see her walking away, heading along the quayside towards the village. He noticed she was still wearing the duffel coat she'd borrowed from Shannon, then his view was blocked as another load of cement was swung ashore from the coaster.

He headed aft. There was one thing he wanted to make sure about before he went ashore.

As usual, Clapper Bell was in the scuba compartment. He was spruced up, obviously ready to go ashore, but instead he was leaning in the doorway, staring out at the harbour with an odd frown on his rugged face.

'You've heard?' asked Carrick.

'Aye. The Old Man just told me.' Bell spoke softly, a puzzled note in his voice. He sighed and tapped a clenched fist aimlessly against the bulkhead metal for a moment. 'It's dam' hard to believe, though.'

'Why?'

Bell grimaced. 'George MacKenzie didn't take chances. An' even if he got into trouble, he was a fair to middlin' swimmer.' He shrugged. 'Still, if your number comes up –'

'You could ask around, find out what maybe did happen,' suggested Carrick.

Bell nodded. 'I will. An' raise a glass or two for him at the same time. Uh – fancy comin' along, sir?'

Carrick made his answer a vague half-promise. A little later, clear of the last of berthing duties, he went ashore. Once he had passed the coaster the quayside quickly became the usual maze of stacked fish boxes and drying nets, of container trucks being loaded and other trucks replenishing boats with fuel oil and crushed ice.

There was prosperity in the air – mixed in with the inevitable odour compounded of fish offal, diesel exhaust and rotting seaweed. Even the big black-backed gulls stalking arrogantly around were as plump as any he'd seen, and the overflowing fish boxes were crammed. Cod and haddock, blue-skinned mackerel, brown-skinned flat fish and the inevitable undersea oddities that came with them were piled along the quay, while the auctioning and price-haggling process went on around them.

But he noticed one other thing as he went along keeping his pace to a casual stroll, eavesdropping on bargainings between skippers and buyers, occasionally stopping to show an apparent interest in another newly landed catch. Fishery Protection uniform could produce different reactions from fishermen, from a friendly nod to blank-faced hostility. Somehow, in a way hard to label, Feanport was different. He was conscious of eyes following him as he passed, of conversations dying. It wasn't hostility.

It was something else, something close to apprehension and yet a couple of times he caught a man looking at him with what could almost have been hope – before the individual concerned turned quickly away and vanished among his companions. Captain Shannon had asked him to smell the air – and the Feanport air reeked of tension.

Rounding the head of the harbour, he slowed again. The dark blue ex-navy launch he'd seen earlier was tied up beside a cluster of line-fishing boats. Her name was the *Sea Whip*. She looked fast and bristled with sophisticated equipment, but he kept going, because something more important had caught his eye ahead, the tide-stained, barnacled edge of a repair slipway.

When he got there and looked down from the edge, the *Rachel* was lying high and dry out of the water with the hole in her port side – a hole big enough to thread a man through – clearly visible. Other spectators, mostly fishermen, were gathered around solemnly inspecting the damage, then he saw Angus Grant climbing the stone steps that led out of the slipway. A man in overalls was with him, they stopped and exchanged a final word at the top, then Grant turned to leave.

As he did, one of the spectators, a fisherman about

Grant's age who had a patch over one eye, laid a hand on his arm and spoke to him in a low voice. Bleakly, tight-lipped, Grant brushed him aside and strode on – then saw Carrick and seemed to hesitate before he came over.

'What's the verdict?' asked Carrick, thumbing down towards the fishing boat.

'It could be worse,' said Grant carefully. 'Two weeks, they say, then I'll be back fishing. The insurance will pay most of the bill.' He glanced round at their audience and raised his voice. 'Aye, two weeks – and I'll be back.'

'I want to talk to you, skipper,' said Carrick quietly. 'Privately.'

'Then you can walk with me.' Grant's bearded, beak-nosed face didn't alter in expression. As they set off, he spoke again, in a slightly friendlier voice. 'Lachie MacLean has my car over at the road beyond the harbourmaster's office – he drove Shona home so she could change her clothes. We're going back to get her, then we'll visit the hospital and see how Willie is.'

They reached the car in a couple of minutes. An old Ford station wagon, it was parked near the foot of a steep curve of road which led up to Feanport village. Lachie MacLean lounged against the driver's door, drinking a can of beer but broke off for a moment to give Carrick a grin. Behind him, a line of empty container trucks were parked on the slope, waiting their turn to come down and load at the quay.

'What is it you want?' asked Grant, stopping.

'Permission for one of our people to have a look at the damage on the *Rachel*,' said Carrick, keeping his manner to a mild disinterest. 'Captain Shannon has the usual routine report to file to Department – what we did, why we did it.'

'He's welcome,' agreed Grant with a minimal nod. 'Anything else?'

'No.' Carrick paused. 'Should there be?'

Grant's eyes flickered. But whatever he'd been going to reply was lost as a hoarse, warning shout rang out from somewhere near. They swung round and saw the squat bulk of the leading container truck rolling silently and driverless down the steep slope above them, heading straight for the parked Ford.

Lachie MacLean had heard the warning too. The fair-haired fishing hand stared open-mouthed for an instant while the truck, a big Volvo unit, silently gathered speed. Then he dropped the beer can and jumped clear for his life.

In almost slow-motion style the massive container truck struck the little station wagon side-on. Sheer weight and momentum carried it on, pushing the Ford ahead, while glass shattered and metal tore and twisted. Then the Ford, still being shoved sideways, hit a large mooring bollard on the quayside. Both vehicles came to a locked halt in a final crunch of metal.

Stunned into silence, Angus Grant stared at the wreckage. The Volvo truck had embedded its nose into what was left of his Ford but still seemed almost undamaged. White-faced at his escape, Lachie MacLean was picking himself up from the ground again while men came hurrying over from several directions. The first to arrive, a slim-built, middle-aged man wearing a sheepskin jacket and black beret, stopped beside Grant and shook his head.

'All I could do was shout,' he said dolefully. 'Sorry, skipper – I saw it start rolling, but all I could do was yell.'

'Thank God you did,' said Grant hoarsely.

'At least no one was hurt,' said the other man. He eyed Carrick. 'I'm John Marsh, from the seaweed plant. You're from the fishery cruiser?'

Carrick nodded, considering Marsh with a new interest. The man who ran the seaweed processing plant for the Vullan family had dark hair, a lined, sallow face and bright, calculating eyes. His accent was far removed from Scotland but was hard to place.

'You saw it happen?' asked Carrick.

'Yes. It just started rolling.' Marsh turned to Angus Grant and shook his head sympathetically. 'You're having a real run of bad luck, skipper.'

'It would have been worse, but for you,' said Grant in a tight voice.

A knot of onlookers had gathered. A fair-haired man in driving overalls pushed his way through them and moistened his lips.

'That's my truck,' he said unhappily. 'But hell, I left the handbrake tight on, so help me.' Then seeing the expression on Grant's face, he took a wary half-step back. 'Look, mister, I'm just trying to say I'm sorry.'

'Where were you?' demanded Grant curtly.

'Talking wi' some of my mates,' said the man defensively. 'That's no crime, is it?' The handbrake must have jumped loose – just one o' those things, right?'

Carrick went past them, eased through the onlookers,

opened the truck door, and swung himself up into the Volvo's driving cab. As he located the handbrake lever John Marsh arrived at the cab door and peered in.

'Go ahead, try it,' invited Marsh. 'You've got a witness.'

Carrick reached down and gave the lever a tug. It tightened a full inch before the ratchet clicked to a halt.

'Bad luck or damned carelessness,' said Marsh flatly. 'Either way, his insurance company won't argue so Skipper Grant is all right.'

Carrick returned the brake lever to its original position and climbed out of the cab again.

'Where were you when the truck started moving?' he asked.

'Over there.' Marsh thumbed towards the quayside then nodded wisely. 'I'm ahead of you, Chief Officer, but you're wrong. There was no one anywhere near it.'

'Accidents happen,' agreed Carrick unemotionally.

'Right.' Marsh slammed the truck door shut for him. 'But don't count on Angus Grant seeing it that way. He gets some strange ideas.'

'I'll remember,' promised Carrick, and left him.

The same cluster of onlookers was still around Angus Grant and the luckless truck driver but Carrick deliberately skirted past them, heading back towards *Marlin*, Then he saw Lachie MacLean ahead, standing at the edge of the quay, staring out across the harbour. His face was drained, his eyes were on the dark blue hull of the *Sea Whip*.

'Feel all right now?' asked Carrick.

MacLean nodded.

'Nice lines,' said Carrick, nodding towards the *Sea Whip*. 'Who owns her?'

'Dorothy Vullan,' said MacLean bleakly.

Carrick blinked. 'Did she come over on it?'

'No, but her husband did,' grated the fishing hand. 'He went to see your captain – Marsh brought him over from the island.'

'Lucky for you,' mused Carrick. 'Marsh probably saved your life.'

'Marsh is all right,' said MacLean curtly. 'A man has to earn a living.'

He turned and walked away.

CHAPTER THREE

The petty officer on gangway watch intercepted Webb Carrick as he stepped aboard *Marlin.* Captain Shannon wanted him to report immediately.

He headed for'ard, to the day cabin below the bridge. On the way, a difference in the fishery cruiser's normal background life-pulse registered and made him smile. The normal purr of the main generator was missing and the slightly higher whine of the auxiliary had taken its place – Andy Shaw was using a chief engineer's prerogative and wasting no time in carrying out the maintenance he'd programmed.

Carrick knocked on the door of the day cabin, heard the usual muffled bark which meant he could enter, and went in. Shannon and a stranger were seated in the cabin's two armchairs, a bottle of Shannon's prized single-malt whisky and two emptied glasses between them on a small table.

'Well timed, mister,' said Shannon, welcoming him with a nod. 'We've a visitor who wanted to meet you.'

'I'm Milne Vullan.' The other man, a tall, lantern-jawed figure who looked in his early fifties rose with athletic ease and held out his hand. 'From what I've heard, Carrick, you did a good job on the *Rachel.'*

Vullan's handshake was a powerful squeeze. He had dark, wavy hair flecked with grey, a rugged, still good-looking face, and wore an open-necked shirt under an old tweed suit which was patched with leather at the elbows.

'It depends on the version you heard,' said Carrick, noticing one thing more – Vullan wore a waterproof diving watch on his left wrist.

'I talked to Shona Grant,' said Vullan easily. 'I'd say she was pretty unbiased.'

Shannon grunted, still in his armchair. 'We've been talking about ballot boxes, mister. Collecting them, how and when – Mr Vullan is local Returning Officer in this damned by-election.'

'Which means being on the sharp end of any complaints,' said Vullan wryly. 'There are votes to gather from half a dozen islands, Carrick. Maybe no more than a couple of hundred votes altogether – but they could be enough to swing the result, so they matter.'

'But we've sorted out a timetable,' shrugged Shannon. His eyes flickered a warning. 'How was your – ah – walk around, mister?'

'Ask Angus Grant,' said Carrick. 'A runaway truck thumped his car while it was lying empty.'

'Grant again?' Vullan winced.

'But nobody hurt,' assured Carrick. 'Your plant manager, John Marsh, was there – he'll tell you about it.'

'No doubt.' Vullan sighed a little and glanced at his watch. 'Still, that man Grant is having his share of woe.' He turned to Shannon and shaped a grin. 'Captain, it's time I got back. I've some fish tanks to tend, or that Witch wife of mine will give me hell.'

'You and I have an invitation, Mr Carrick,' said Shannon getting to his feet. 'We're invited to Fean House tonight for a meal, if you can find a clean shirt.'

'I'd like that,' agreed Carrick. 'And I'll borrow the shirt.'

Vullan chuckled a little. 'It'll just be family, Carrick. I'll expect you both around eight – will I send a boat over, Captain?'

Shannon seemed to consider for a moment, then shook his head. 'We'll just arrive.'

Vullan shook hands with them both again, and left.

'And I'm glad that's over,' said Shannon softly once the cabin door had closed. He flopped back into his chair, topped up his glass from the bottle, then remembered Carrick. 'Get a glass of your own, mister. Then sit down – make the place look tidier.'

Carrick fetched a spare glass from a locker beside Shannon's old leather-topped desk. Twice as big as Carrick's cramped quarters, the day cabin had one startling feature – bright chintz curtains at the portholes, contributed by Captain Shannon's wife. *Marlin*'s commander loathed them almost as much as her other contribution, a rubber plant which moped in a corner and refused to die, but he seemed to lack the courage to get rid of them.

The rest, from spotless white paintwork to gleaming brass, was practical and comfortable. A roll pendulum and repeater compass hung above the desk. A bookshelf was crammed with Fishery Department handbooks and most of one bulkhead was occupied by a taped-up spread of Admiralty chart on which Shannon had outlined the new

British two-hundred-mile exclusive fishing limits with a black felt-tip pen.

Black for mourning, decided Carrick. The new fishing limits had been decreed by the politicians, but the fishery cruiser captains were still waiting for the politicians to explain how, without major air support, you kept tabs on all that went on within that two-hundred-mile limit in anything more than pretend style.

Pouring himself a drink from the bottle, he kept it modest in size and didn't look for water. James Shannon regarded adding water to whisky as a sacrilege to be compared with being rude about the Queen or being seasick on his bridge.

'All right,' said Shannon brusquely as soon as Carrick was seated. 'Let's have it. I asked you to sniff the air. It sounds like your nose got you into trouble.'

'If you mean Grant's car being wrecked it had all the looks of an accident,' said Carrick carefully. 'The rest of it – well, it's hard to label. A smell, like you said. But –' He shrugged, then, flatly and factually, told what had happened.

When he'd finished, Shannon gave a slow nod then sat silent for a spell, nursing his glass between his stubby fingers. Then at last he gave a grunt.

'Doesn't help much, does it?' He scowled at the black-lined chart, a handy focus for his thoughts. 'Seen Clapper Bell?'

'Not since he went ashore.'

'He may pick up something,' said Shannon hopefully. 'But now we've got Vullan – the way he came aboard, almost as soon as we'd berthed, could be straightforward. He brought the blank voting papers and the sealed ballot boxes for delivery to the islands. But on the other hand he tried hard to find out if there was any other reason for us coming to Feanport.'

'What about tonight's invitation?' posed Carrick.

'It's the tradition when a fishery cruiser arrives, like I told you.' Shannon sipped a modicum of whisky and rinsed it around his mouth before he swallowed. 'Still, whatever's going on, get one thing straight. Vullan is no fool – even if his wife usually overshadows him. He ended up commanding a destroyer in World War Two. Now he does high-powered consultant work in marine biology.' His eyes strayed to the limits chart again. 'That includes having advised half a dozen Government commissions on fish-stock breeding areas. Don't jump to any wrong conclusions about him.'

'But we go tonight?' pressed Carrick.

'I wouldn't miss the chance,' said Shannon. A wisp of a smile crossed his round, bearded face. 'Mister, we may learn something, we may not – but they keep a damned good whisky at Fean House. That's one kind of witchcraft I'll always respect.'

It was about an hour later when Carrick went ashore again and the scene around the harbour had changed considerably.

Dusk was edging in from the sea The sky had acquired a dull edge of grey cloud to the north-west, which might mean rain or snow before morning, and the wind seemed to have freshened. A few fishing boats were murmuring out for a night's work, pitching a little in the swell as they cleared the breakwater, but the rest lay deserted at their berths. The fish buyers and the container trucks had gone, and the harbour had a sleepy air as if it was resting.

He had two good reasons for going ashore. One was to locate Clapper Bell, who still hadn't returned from his wanderings and the other was to escape from Jumbo Wills, who was moaning about being stuck aboard as duty officer.

At the end of the harbour he reached the place where Angus Grant's station wagon had been demolished by the runaway truck. Everything had been cleared and only a powdering of glass remained to hint at what had happened. Going on, Carrick toiled up the gradient to the start of the village, and had his first real close-up view of Feanport.

Clinging to the rising ground, it amounted to a few tight, narrow streets of old stone cottages, with black slate roofs. Here and there naked granite rock jutted out between the buildings and broke the pattern. Occasionally there was a larger structure and higher up the hill, not much more than a silhouette in the fading light, he saw a church and a small graveyard.

He walked along, the scent of peat-smoke in his nostrils, the contrast of the TV aerials which cluttered the cottage roofs and the sight of a brightly lit shop window filled with refrigerators and washing machines bringing a slight smile to his lips. The only signs of the coming by-election were a few political posters peeling from walls.

A voice hailed him and he stopped as another figure in Fishery Protection uniform crossed the street to join him. It was Ferguson, and *Marlin*'s junior second mate looked even more pinch-faced than usual in the greying dusk.

'Doing the town?' asked Ferguson sarcastically. 'I found a notice that says the British Legion pipe band have a practice in the village hall tonight. Add a couple of bars and a fishermen's co-operative store with a liquor licence, and you've heard it all.'

'Rent a kilt somewhere,' said Carrick mildly. 'You'd look good in a pipe band – the drum major could twirl you or something.' He glanced up and down the little street, which was almost deserted. 'Seen Clapper Bell?'

Ferguson scowled. 'Yes, damn his insolence.'

'Meaning?'

'You know him,' answered Ferguson bleakly. 'One day I'll have him on report before the Old Man. But if you want him, he was in the Anchor Watch – it's a bar in the next street on your left.'

Ferguson stalked off, and Carrick moved on past a small single-storey building which had a sign which said Cottage Hospital. Just ahead, an old truck clattered out of a side street and turned down towards the harbour.

'Fishery snoop,' yelled the driver from the open cab window, then made a grating gear-change as he pulled away.

Unperturbed, Carrick glanced after the truck then paused. On the other side of the street a man had just slipped quickly into the shelter of a shop doorway. It was the little man with an eye-patch he'd seen trying to talk to Angus Grant at the harbour. Deliberately, casually, Carrick stuck his hands in his pockets and turned up the side street.

Once he'd rounded the next corner he stopped and made a pretence of studying another collection of neglected election posters, waiting. After a moment, the little man with the eye-patch hurried round, saw him, and kept going. But he stopped again, further along the street, apparently interested in another shop-window.

Casually, Carrick walked on, reached him, and stopped. The man kept his attention on the window display, though he'd chosen badly. It was a women's hairdressing salon, and as Carrick didn't move the man suddenly turned, almost dived away, and headed back the way he had come. For a moment Carrick thought of reversing the process and following him, but the Anchor Watch bar was just a little way along the street and he settled for that.

The Anchor Watch was small, the ceiling low, the woodwork dark with age and varnish, and the air was stale with tobacco smoke. Carrick paused inside the door, where the linoleum floor covering was so old the pattern had almost vanished, saw a cluster of fishermen playing darts in a corner, glanced round the rest of the customers, then spotted Clapper Bell elbowed up at the bar.

'I'm orderin',' said Bell with a slight grin as Carrick joined him. 'Name it.'

'Whisky,' Carrick told the wizened barman, who had just dumped two pint mugs of beer in front of the red-haired bo'sun. 'All right, Clapper, since when did you buy drinks for anyone?'

'It happens sometimes,' said Bell. As the barman turned for the whisky, he added quietly, 'An' I'd call this lubrication. I'm drinkin' with the harbourmaster, an old josser called Morrison. He's talkative, sir.'

'Then I'll do the buying.' Carrick paid for the drinks as the whisky arrived. But as Bell lifted the beer mugs, he stopped him. 'What about your pal the village constable? Heard anything?'

Bell shook his head, his eyes bleak for a moment. 'Not much more than that he went fishin' an' didn't come back. His body an' the boat were washed up near Broch Point.'

'Talked to his replacement?' queried Carrick.

'He hasn't arrived yet,' said Bell derisively. 'The cop in the next village is coverin', but that means he's on the end of a telephone twenty miles away.' He glanced past Carrick. 'My punter's gettin' restive, sir.'

They took the drinks across to a table where a red-cheeked, elderly man wearing a dark blue donkey jacket sat with a peaked cap and a couple of empty beer glasses in front of him. Clapper Bell kept the introductions brief – Shuggy Morrison was a naval pensioner who regarded being harbourmaster at Feanport as a suitably non-strenuous way of picking up some extra money.

'Though there's a wee bit excitement now and again,' he admitted, surfacing from his new drink and wiping the beer suds from his upper lip. 'Like the *Rachel* coming in today.'

'Tricky for you,' said Bell solemnly and gave Carrick a

cautionary glance. 'But you were sayin' some of the boats are in the money, right?'

Morrison nodded. 'The boats wi' sensible skippers, who know where to fish.' He paused and winked slyly. 'Or maybe I mean wi' skippers who'll do what they're told. It can be the same thing, eh?'

'Would Angus Grant agree?' asked Carrick bluntly.

'Him?' Shuggy Morrison hesitated and shrugged. 'You won't find heather growing out o' my ears – I'm from Glasgow, like your bo'sun. But I still won't go feuding wi' the Witch of the Isles the way he does.'

'That began a long time ago,' mused Carrick.

'Before I came,' agreed Morrison. He wheezed a wary chuckle. 'I'm not saying she scares me. I haven't been scared of a woman since my wife ran off with a window-cleaner. But there's good luck and bad luck, and Grant's boat is out there wi' a damned great hole in it.'

Carrick caught himself wishing for a cigarette, sighed for the pack taped to his cabin mirror, and fought down the momentary craving.

'What started their quarrel?' he asked.

'Domestic, something to do wi' Grant's wife when she was alive,' shrugged Morrison. 'Don't ask me why it flared up again, except he hasn't had much fishing luck lately. But even so –'

'Even so, what?' said Carrick grimly.

Morrison looked around the bar cautiously, then lowered his voice. 'Like I said, I'm not one of your superstitious hairy Highlanders, right? But if I was, then I'd have gone a damned sight more carefully than Grant did. Because I'd have thought about what happened to the last man to start a feud wi' that woman.' He grimaced. 'That was the village constable, and he drowned.'

'George MacKenzie?' Clapper Bell stared at him, then swore angrily. 'You didn't tell me that!'

'Did you ask me?' Morrison scowled nervously, finished his beer in a quick series of gulps, and pushed back his chair. 'I'm going – thanks for the drink.'

'Not yet.' Clapper Bell grabbed him by the arm.

'I'm not lookin' for trouble,' protested Morrison, then gave a low yelp as Bell's grip tightened.

'Trouble just found you,' said Carrick stonily. 'You're staying, till we hear the rest.'

Licking his lips, the elderly harbourmaster glanced

around. But the darts match was still in full swing and no one else in the bar seemed in the slightest way interested in what was happening to him.

'All right,' he surrendered with a wheeze. 'The gossip around the harbour is that MacKenzie got mad because the Vullan woman complained to his bosses about somethin' he'd done and landed him in trouble. Then – well, he began asking questions around the harbour. Questions about her boat, the *Sea Whip* and where people had seen it. He said he was going to get his own back.' The man paused and looked at them earnestly. 'So help me, that's all I know.'

'And before MacKenzie?' grated Clapper Bell.

'You mean – others?' Morrison gave a nervous grimace. 'A few idiots aroun' the harbour are blaming her for every damned thing from the odd storm at sea to their girl friends going sour. But that's only started now.'

'Let him go, Clapper,' said Carrick wearily.

'I just do my job,' said Morrison, scrambling to his feet as Bell released his grip. 'Do it, and keep my nose clean. Remember that.'

'I'll arrange a vote of thanks,' said Carrick.

Barely managing a muttered good-bye, the man hurried to the Anchor Watch's door and left. As the door slammed shut Clapper Bell scratched his chin and didn't try to hide his bewilderment.

'What the hell did George MacKenzie get himself into?' he asked in a note of disbelief.

'Maybe I can ask Dorothy Vullan,' said Carrick. 'The Old Man's taking me to meet her tonight.'

'A little bit o' witchcraft wouldn't do our captain any harm,' grunted Bell. 'But that business about the *Sea Whip* –'

'Could mean anything or nothing, so don't start building fancy theories.' Finishing his drink, Carrick pointed a finger. 'Why is Ferguson making complaining noises about you?'

'That?' Bell's face twisted into an expression of innocence. 'I just exchanged a private opinion or two with him, sir. If an officer starts accusin' you of runnin' a poker school in the galley, but agrees he can't prove it –'

'Then a wise man closes the game down fast,' said Carrick wearily. 'Or he moves it on. Either way, I don't want to know. I've more to worry about.'

'Sir.' Bell gave a penitent nod, then winked. 'But there's no harm in me thinkin' he's an old woman, is there?'

Carrick gave up, thumbed him to his feet, and they headed for the door. Several of the Anchor Watch's customers watched them go, a couple gave a brief, half-friendly nod of greeting, but none said a word.

Dusk had given way to dark outside, the sky had completely clouded over, and the temperature seemed to have fallen several degrees. But Feanport had a peaceful, tranquil air. Only an occasional car passed the two Fishery Protection men as they headed in the direction of the harbour through the quiet streets.

A dog was barking somewhere in the distance. Music and laughter came from some of the cottages, a baby was crying in another. The whole atmosphere was soothing and Clapper Bell began humming a tune under his breath.

But as they came near to the cottage hospital there was a sudden shout and the sound of running feet. A moment later a figure shot out of a lane just ahead and hesitated under the glare of a street lamp. It was Donnie MacLean, the third of the *Rachel*'s fishing hands – and as he tried to start running again two figures pounced out of the lane and grabbed him. Something swung under the light, MacLean went limp, and the two men began dragging him back into the lane.

Clapper Bell charged forward, Carrick pounding along beside him. A third man appeared at the mouth of the lane, saw them, called a warning, and MacLean was abandoned, falling to the ground.

Tackling the figure nearest him, Carrick dodged a kick, slammed a fist into the man's middle, and heard a howl and a thud. Clapper Bell had grabbed his first choice and had literally picked him up and thrown him against the nearest wall.

While Bell swung round to challenge the third figure, Carrick's man came in again, cursing. This time Carrick circled warily as he saw the beer-can ring-pulls which his opponent wore on each fist like knuckle-dusters – the kind of knuckle-dusters which could rip open a man's face.

Feinting, he faked a stumble, lured the man on, then catapulted forward. His shoulder took his opponent hard in the chest, they went down together, rolled, and he felt the cloth of his jacket tear as a slashing blow from the ring-pulls grazed his side. Carrick countered with a flat-edged hand-jab which smashed across the man's mouth – then as the man squealed and scrambled clear, another shout rang out.

Suddenly, as suddenly as they'd appeared, all three men ran back up the lane and disappeared into the darkness. As Carrick got up, Clapper Bell joined him, panting a little but grinning, and thumbed at the lane.

'Do we go after them?' he asked.

'No chance. We'd be chasing our tails.' Carrick turned and stooped over Donnie MacLean who was lying groaning. 'Help me get him up.'

Between them, they got the fishing hand to his feet and he managed to stay that way, leaning against a wall.

'You'll live, son,' said Clapper Bell cheerfully. 'You took a thump on the head an' a kick in the slats, that's all.'

'All?' MacLean grimaced, clung to the wall, and took a deep, painful breath. 'Thanks for – well, being around.'

'Recognize them?' asked Carrick.

'No.' MacLean took a step away from the wall, swayed on his feet, but stayed upright. 'They – they jumped me in the lane. I'd been to see my brother at the cottage hospital.'

'You nearly booked the bed next to him,' grunted Clapper Bell. 'They were ready to make it a ring-pull job – the doctor who patched you would have needed a sewing machine.'

'But why?' demanded Carrick. He didn't get an answer and tried again. 'You must have an idea, Donnie'

'Drunks,' said MacLean vaguely, and shook his head. 'Drunks or head-bangers off one o' the outside boats in the harbour. Let's just forget it, right?'

'Forget it?' Clapper Bell swore incredulously.

'Easier, always is.' The fishing hand nodded earnestly. 'I'm okay, an' I live just at the top of the lane – my cousin Lachie is in the house, so no problems.'

'If that's the way you want it,' agreed Carrick neutrally. 'How is brother Willie getting on?'

'Fine – bandaged up, but fine,' said Donnie MacLean quickly. 'They say he can get out tomorrow. Uh – I'll get home now.'

'But we'll make sure you get there,' said Carrick.

They went with him, ignoring his protesting noises. The lane snaked its way up through the village and the MacLean cottage, last in a row, overlooked bare hillside. The fishing hand opened the door and looked embarrassed.

'Thanks again,' he said quickly. 'Thanks and – well, forget it, like I asked.'

He'd gone inside and the door was closed before they could reply.

'Gratitude, sheer gratitude,' said Clapper Bell caustically. 'Take a look at what one o' his little pals dropped.'

The home-made cosh he handed Carrick was a crude affair made from lead piping bound with electrical flex and swinging from a piece of knotted rope.

'Primitive,' said Carrick, swinging it speculatively. 'But the weight's right.'

'Spot on,' grunted Bell. Then he realized Carrick was staring at something above the cottage door, took a half-step nearer, peered up, and swore softly.

'Rowan,' agreed Carrick.

A fresh branch of rowan was nailed above the doorway. Donnie MacLean might say he didn't know who had attacked him or why, but he'd already taken out insurance of a different kind.

Ninety minutes later – ninety minutes that passed quickly – Webb Carrick stepped ashore on Fean Island for the first time.

Earlier, when he had returned to *Marlin* at the harbour, he had again brought Captain Shannon up to date with Clapper Bell beside him to give the occasional growl of confirmation. None of it had improved Shannon's mood and at the end they'd learned why.

Dragged away from repairing the main generator, Andy Shaw had visited the *Rachel* on the harbour slipway. But the fishery cruiser's chief engineer had returned empty-handed.

'He'll take bets that someone got there ahead of him,' snarled Shannon. 'There's just that damned hole in her side – and one or two bits of broken metal that don't matter a damn. The valve head, even the feed pipes to the galley stove have gone. Destroyed in the explosion or gone overboard – like hell they were.'

Carrick knew that Shannon's real wrath was that he hadn't anticipated it. But later, once he'd washed and changed for their visit to Fean Island, he returned on deck to find *Marlin*'s commander in a more amiable mood and a minor surprise waiting. The fishery cruiser's brand-new patrol launch had been lowered and was ready to take them on the short trip across to the island.

'I was going to use one of the small boats, then I decided to put on a show,' said Shannon gruffly. 'Just you and I, mister – call it a little bit of bluff for general benefit.'

They climbed down a ladder, got aboard, and Shannon took the controls while Carrick cast off. Twenty-five-feet long and with a high-performance engine, the patrol launch rated as Shannon's newest toy and he guarded it like a secret weapon. Twin screws gave the slim-lined hull a speed well in excess of Marlin's thrusting thirty knots – but when she went snarling out of the harbour a few minutes later she made a lot of noise and wash but was still throttled well back from maximum.

Shannon kept things that way, even once they were clear of the harbour breakwater. Standing beside him in the cockpit, Carrick decided it was a foxy move – plenty of eyes would have watched them leave, plenty of experienced fishermen would have been very interested in the patrol launch's performance. But he could guess their verdict, that the patrol launch was just another moderately fast boat that could be matched and probably beaten by quite a few local craft.

Including Vullan's *Sea Whip*. The thought was in his mind as the short trip to the island was completed and the patrol launch slowed, coming in towards the jetty below Fean House. The *Sea Whip* was there, tied up for the night beside a couple of smaller boats, and as the patrol launch murmured in beside her two figures appeared on the jetty alongside and hailed a greeting.

They were Milne Vullan and John Marsh, and they took the mooring lines, then waited in the darkness until Shannon and Carrick joined them.

From the jetty, they were led up the flight of worn stone steps that led to the dark silhouette of Fean House then round and across a patch of overgrown garden to the front of the house, where several of the windows were brightly lit. The door lay open and a moment later they were in the warmth of the house.

'Good evening, Captain Shannon,' said a woman's husky voice. 'It's good to see you again. Introduce me to your friend.'

Mrs Dorothy Mary Fergus MacDonald Vullan, hereditary Witch of the Isles, stood in the big hall of Fean House, her back to a stone fireplace where enough driftwood blazed to roast any self-respecting ox and smiled at her guests.

'You look well, Mrs Vullan,' said Captain Shannon awkwardly.

It was probably as much of a compliment as he'd paid a woman in years, but in Dorothy Vullan's case, it was justified. As Shannon muttered an introduction, Carrick adjusted to his initial surprise.

The Witch of the Isles was a woman in her early fifties, but that was incidental. Tall and straight-shouldered, with short, copper-bronze hair which glinted like flame in the firelight, she had a figure most women half her age would have been proud to possess. Her eyes were green, her face had a quality about it which ignored the first tiny lines of age, and she wore an ankle-length green velvet skirt with a simple white shirt-blouse and a chunky gold-link necklace. Her only other jewellery was her wedding ring.

'I'm glad you could come too, Chief Officer,' she said with a twinkle as they shook hands. Then she glanced past him. 'Stop hiding back there, Shona.'

'Who's hiding?' protested Shona Grant.

Carrick hadn't seen her till then. She came over to join them from behind a leather-topped cocktail bar, where she'd been laying out glasses. Her long chestnut hair was caught back by a silver clasp and she wore a tailored suede jacket over black velvet slacks and a flame-coloured blouse. Dorothy Vullan turned her attention back to Shannon, leaving them alone for a moment.

'Don't look quite so surprised,' murmured Shona. 'I got invited, the same way you did.'

'I'll bet that made your father happy,' said Carrick dryly.

'He's having to learn I make my own decisions.' Her grey eyes clouded for a moment, then her mood brightened again. 'Well, what do you think of our Witch of the Isles?'

'She's – well, not what I expected,' admitted Carrick. 'I'm impressed.'

'Go on,' urged Dorothy Vullan's voice unexpectedly. She had come up behind him and looked amused. A wary-faced Captain Shannon was by her side. 'How do you feel about witches, Chief Officer?'

'Right now I feel I must have read the wrong comic books at school,' he said solemnly.

She liked that and gave a husky chuckle.

'Being a witch can be fun – sometimes,' she declared. 'But it can have its disadvantages too – ask my ancestors. Most of them met some kind of nasty end.'

'Most of them deserved it. But I've no complaints,' said Milne Vullan, who had overheard. Coming over from where he'd been standing with Marsh, he laid a hand on her shoulder and gave her a look of genuine affection. 'No complaints at all – not yet, anyway.'

'He's the tolerant kind,' explained Dorothy Vullan. 'That's why I married him. Milne, while you're in that kind of mood how about pouring some drinks?'

The talk became general for a spell. Marsh helped Vullan with the drinks while Dorothy Vullan took Shannon and Carrick on a guided tour round the collection of old banners, glinting weaponry and paintings which decorated the stone walls of the hall.

'You've seen most of this before, captain, I know,' she said almost apologetically. 'But I enjoy doing it – when a house has been lived in for over three hundred years it collects history like cobwebs.'

'Except for Bonnie Prince Charlie,' murmured Shona Grant mildly.

'Yes, we missed out there,' admitted Dorothy Vullan sadly. 'The Witch of that time had the kind of reputation that frightened him off.'

'It wouldn't happen now,' said John Marsh, offering her a drink.

'I wouldn't be too sure.' Her mouth tightened for a moment, then she took the glass from him, sipped, returned to her theme. 'Take a good look at these broadswords above the fireplace, Mr Carrick. They were used at Culloden – on the losing side.'

They ate a little later, at an oval table in a wood-panelled dining room, the walls decorated with heavily framed paintings of old sailing ship scenes. The table sparkled with crystal and silver, but Dorothy Vullan served the food from a heated trolley – Fean House's domestic help came from the village by day and were back there by nightfall.

It was a meal in the Highland tradition, from game soup to grilled venison and finishing with a selection of island cheeses and tiny oatmeal bannocks. Placed next to Shona Grant and facing Shannon across the table, Carrick learned several things about their hosts and Marsh from the general conversation.

Milne Vullan and the Witch of the Isles had met and married while he'd been a young naval officer. Now he used Fean House as a base for his marine consultancy work and also helped Dorothy Vullan run a hotch-potch of family business interests around the Feanport area – most of them, he claimed ruefully, anything but profit-making. John Marsh, who stayed quiet most of the meal, listening, smiling, but seldom joining in the conversation, lived alone in a cottage at the south end of Fean Island.

His coming to Feanport was recent though, as Vullan explained, he and Marsh had known each other since wartime days. Marsh had come north on a visit after returning to Britain after a spell of working abroad and had ended up staying on to manage the seaweed plant.

'Strange things happen up here.' A slight smile on his lips, Marsh glanced along the table at Dorothy Vullan. 'Maybe somebody heaved a spell in my direction.'

An odd look passed between Dorothy Vullan and her husband and her manner held an underlying touch of frost when she answered.

'I certainly wasn't involved,' she said deliberately.

A flush showed on Marsh's lined, sallow face. Making a throat-clearing noise, Captain Shannon bridged the awkward silence that followed.

'As election campaigns go, I wouldn't call the one around here a fireball affair,' he said heavily. 'What's wrong? Did we arrive too late – or too early?'

'Nobody cares,' suggested Milne Vullan, looking relieved at the switch in conversation. 'Well' – his glance switched to Shona Grant, who gave him a mock scowl – 'hardly anyone. You'll always find a few of the political faithful around. Shona for one.'

'If you mean one of the reasons I'm home is so I can vote on Friday, that's right,' said the girl with an unexpected vigour. 'It's not my fault most of Feanport and the islands, in fact the whole Lochard constituency, would vote for a stuffed haggis if it wore the right party label.'

'There speaks a bright-eyed, bushy-tailed Scottish Nationalist – home rule for Feanport, but don't ask her to stay there,' said Dorothy Vullan good-naturedly. 'But Shona's speaking the truth. Bringing a political bandwagon up here is a waste of time. Even the candidates know it – about the most they've done here is pass through quickly.'

'You mean none of them have come wooing the Witch of the Isles?' Shannon helped himself to more wine and looked surprised. 'I'd have done it, then put you to work drumming up support.'

'I wouldn't do them much good.' Dorothy Vullan gave a slight grimace. 'Don't confuse inherited notoriety with popularity, Captain. Though I'm afraid I'm even a disappointment as a witch.' She saw Carrick raise a quizzical eyebrow and shook her head. 'I used to try very hard casting spells when I was a child, just to see if it worked. It never did.'

'From what I can make out, the old witches in Dorothy's family really used a mixture of folk medicine and psychology,' said Milne Vullan indulgently. 'Slip a man something that will purge his bowels and you're all set to scare the hell out of him.'

'What about today?' asked Carrick quietly. He saw Shannon give the faintest of nods and went on. 'Some of the fishermen around Feanport still seem to reckon the Witch of the Isles can guide a man to a good catch – if she wants.'

Dorothy Vullan had a coffee cup halfway to her lips. She set it down slowly.

'Who told you that?' she asked, the expression in her green eyes hard to read.

'Sounds like some of your crew have been drinking ashore, Carrick,' said John Marsh with a grunt that wasn't quite a laugh.

'Gossip,' agreed Carrick. 'But it wasn't about the old days – it was about now.'

'I know about it,' said Dorothy Vullan almost curtly. 'I –'

'I think maybe Milne is the one who should explain it,' cut in Marsh. He glanced at Milne Vullan. 'I warned you about those stories, didn't I?'

'Yes.' Vullan gave a resigned sigh and ran a hand through his dark hair. 'I'd planned to tell you a little about it anyway, Captain Shannon. In fact, I can do better than that – I can show you the basics. All that has been happening is that I've been playing around with a few fishing ideas and occasionally getting one or two of the local skippers to co-operate.' He turned to his wife. 'We could do it right now.'

'If you want.' She nodded her agreement. 'I'll stay here and clear up.'

'And I'll make that my cue to say good night,' said Marsh. Pushing back his chair, he added, 'I've some paper-work lying at the cottage, Milne. You don't mind?'

'No, go ahead,' agreed Vullan. 'Shona, you'll come along?'

She nodded.

'Good,' he said, and gave a slight smile. 'You've seen some of it before, but not everything.'

They rose from the table and, once Marsh had gone, Dorothy Vullan began tidying while her husband led the others out of the room. They went along a corridor and down a flight of stairs, then stopped while Vullan opened a door and flicked on some lights.

'My workshop,' he said dryly, beckoning them to enter.

It was a long, narrow basement filled with fish tanks, equipment racks and laboratory benches. The neon tube lights shone down on a large table in the middle of it all where there was a three-dimensional undersea contour map of the waters around Feanport. A web of electrical cabling linked a series of control panels to some of the fish tanks and in the tanks, disturbed by the lights, scores of fish of all sizes were darting around.

Looking around, Carrick gave a silent whistle of appreciation. It was like being shown a Noah's Ark of the marine life of the Scottish west coast – from cod and dogfish to herring and tiny sprats, the collection was about as comprehensive as any he'd seen.

'Don't ask me for a population figure. It keeps changing.' Vullan gave a tank a tap with his fingers and a large crab stalked across the gravel bottom to investigate then turned away. 'I've got the usual pumps and filters to keep the sea water environment stabilized.'

'I knew you had a laboratory,' said Shannon, and gave an appreciative grunt. 'But I didn't expect this.'

'I don't bring many people down here.' Vullan couldn't keep the pride from his voice. 'This was old, empty cellarage when I started – though I'm afraid it had other uses too. Some of my wife's ancestors seem to have had nasty habits. When I knocked down one wall I found an old, bricked-up dungeon and a full set of chains and manacles.'

'No skeletons?' asked Carrick mildly.

The tall, dark-haired man grinned sourly. 'No. But the

other thing I did find in another corner was a dump of Victorian liquor bottles. Dorothy's great-grandmother was inclined that way. Remember I showed you them, Shona?'

'Will I ever forget?' She chuckled at the memory. 'Yet the story goes everyone thought she was teetotal.'

'They're the worst kind,' said Shannon judiciously. He strode forward, inspected the contour map for a moment, then faced Vullan, his manner friendly but business-like. 'So – how much help have you been giving the Feanport boats?'

Vullan frowned. 'You make it seem like a regular arrangement. It isn't.'

'But?'

'It'll sound like a lecture,' warned Vullan grimly.

'Go on,' nodded Shannon. 'I'm interested enough.'

'All right.' Vullan gestured towards the tanks. 'My speciality is studying the behaviour patterns of fish stock. That means taking any number of factors into account – sea temperature, seasonal feeding, migatory spawning patterns, the rest. Then – well, it's possible to examine what happens if you add outside, artificial factors.'

'Around Feanport?' asked Carrick bluntly.

Vullan nodded. 'In the ordinary way, the local skippers know the fishing grounds around here well enough without any advice from me. What happens is I occasionally suggest where and when a skipper should try his nets – to help me.' He smiled slightly. 'They usually find it profitable.'

Crossing to one of the control panels, he fingered a switch. A large flatfish suddenly exploded up from the sandy bottom of the nearest tank and swam around furiously before gradually settling again.

'Party tricks,' said Vullan unemotionally. 'Here's another one.'

He touched switches again and a bright red light appeared at the far end of a long tank. Immediately a score of silvery mackerel rushed towards the spot – but as they arrived, a cold blue beam took the place of the red and the fish scattered away from it.

'Basic stuff.' Vullan switched off almost apologetically. 'A very small electrical charge will bring any fish off the bottom in a hurry. Different coloured lighting can attract or repel, suggest food or discomfort – and, of course, these are laboratory fish, educated fish. I can build up laboratory theory here, I can go out with the *Sea Whip* and take things a stage further. But if I want any kind of practical small-scale trial I need outside help – fishing skippers.'

Carrick and Shannon exchanged a glance, sharing a silent understanding.

Science had been moving into fishing for some time. There were already forecasts that in a few years the old, relatively haphazard techniques of trawling and netting could be wiped away.

Almost every civilized country with a fishing industry was involved. Shrimp boats over in the Gulf of Mexico had been experimenting for years with electrical fishing – using electrically charged gear to tickle the shrimps out of their sand holes into the nets. French scientists had developed a system for stunning sardine shoals then suction-pumping them aboard catcher boats. The West Germans were working on electrified trawling for eels, the Dutch and Belgians had sea farming projects, the Russians, Poles and East Germans all had their own programmes.

'You know the main research patterns, I imagine,' said Vullan, as if reading their minds. 'What I'm working on is a possible next-stage development. Call it fish-herding if you like – trying to get them to go where the nets are waiting.'

'That has been tried,' said Shannon slowly.

'I'm not saying it's totally original,' declared Vullan. 'But I can go out in the *Sea Whip,* pay out a line of fairly simple electrical packs astern, and know that I'm going to move a lot of fish in a certain direction.'

'How much of this have you explained to the Feanport skippers?' asked Carrick, frowning.

'I've tried. Some seem to understand, but the others –' Vullan stopped there and shrugged. 'How far would your own belief stretch, Chief Officer? Suppose I told you of a man who can train haddock to swim in races, a dozen at a time, as if they were track stars? Or of someone else who can ring a bell at the stern of a boat and have cod come queueing to feed from his hand?'

'I'd believe you – I've seen you do both,' said Shona softly. She faced Carrick and Shannon. 'It was years ago, when I was a child – I thought it was magic.'

'Maybe some people still think that way,' said Shannon soberly.

'It's possible,' conceded Vullan. Then, suddenly he

seemed to deliberately brush the problem aside. 'Captain, there's more I'd like you to see.'

They spent another half-hour in the basement 'workshop' while Vullan invited them to admire everything from a giant lobster called Fred to scale models of experimental trawling gear. There was no chance to get him talking about the fish herding trials again and at last they were led back upstairs and rejoined Dorothy Vullan.

Shannon shook his head at the offer of another drink and glanced at his wristwatch.

'It's time Carrick and I were getting back.' He turned to Shona. 'Miss Grant, did you bring a boat over?'

She shook her head. 'John Marsh came over with a dinghy and collected me.'

'Then we'll give you a lift back to the harbour – if you want that.'

'Please.' She smiled her thanks.

Milne Vullan brought her coat, a white-coloured waterproof, then as they went towards the door of the house Dorothy Vullan suddenly laid a hand on Shannon's arm and stopped him.

'Captain, I want to ask you something,' she said bluntly, a proud, handsome woman with a glint of determination in her eyes. 'You've talked about collecting those ballot boxes from the islands. But is there any other reason why your ship has come to Feanport?'

'No.' Shannon eyed her gravely. 'Should there be?'

'Gossip.' The Witch of the Isles ignored her husband's mutter of protest. 'Well, Captain?'

Shannon's round, plump face reddened beneath his beard. Then he scowled at Milne Vullan.

'Your wife is a damned attractive woman,' he said heavily. 'Tell her not to be a damned fool.'

There was silence in the hallway for a moment, then Dorothy Vullan gave a sigh.

'Thank you, Captain,' she said quietly. 'We'll walk down to the jetty with you.'

Still looking concerned, Milne Vullan nodded and opened the front door. They left the house, went out into the dark, chill night, and started towards the steps that led down to the jetty.

Something moved in the shadows ahead of them, beside a patch of bush, and became the vague shape of a man.

'Who's there?' called Milne Vullan, halting.

The blast of a shotgun answered him. The charge snarled over their heads, smashing into the stonework of Fean House, then the figure had spun round and was running off into the darkness.

CHAPTER FOUR

The common twelve-bore shotgun fires a load that can cut a man in half at fifteen yards, kill him less messily at up to forty yards, and still blind or maim him for life at seventy yards. The three-inch cartridge carries an ounce of lead shot, with a killing 'spread' of about a yard.

Usually, too, it is either a double-barrelled weapon or a five-shot pump-action repeater. The last thought had been the one which had sent Carrick flat on the ground, pulling Shona Grant with him, as the shot lashed over their heads. He'd seen Milne Vullan practically throw his wife behind a cement flower trough and drop down after her while Shannon took a speedy, totally undignified dive in the opposite direction.

But there hadn't been a second shot. Instead, Carrick listened for a moment to the sound of the gunman crashing through the bushes as he ran away. Then, taking a deep breath of relief, he scrambled to his feet again and helped Shona up.

The others were up again too. Unbelievably, they were unhurt if he discounted a graze on Dorothy Vullan's arms where she'd fallen. Shannon was cursing in a voice that would have subdued a hurricane, Shona kept a grip of Carrick's arm, and it was Vullan, staring into the darkness where the figure had vanished, who made the first move.

'Let's get after the maniac,' he said hoarsely, starting forward.

'No,' Shannon stopped him. 'Get your wife and the girl in the house. He could change his mind and come back.' The small, bearded figure turned to Carrick, rasped a quick, curt order. 'Look around, mister. But carefully – don't get your head blown off.'

Carrick nodded, gave Shona Grant a quick grimace that was meant to be reassuring, and set off.

There was a well-worn pathway beyond the bushes and he followed it at a cautious lope through more bush and scrub, every sense alert for the slightest sight or sound of the man he was pursuing, not at all certain what he'd do if he met him. Then, as the path almost petered out at a jagged stretch of rock, he saw something glint on the ground just ahead and picked up a used shotgun cartridge.

So the man had stopped to reload. Stomach tightening at the thought, he shoved the cartridge in his pocket and went on.

The path went through more scrub, then took a sudden dip and he realized it was heading towards the shore. A moment later, he heard pebbles rattle somewhere not far ahead, reached the end of the scrub, and looked down a bare slope.

A figure was scrambling along the slope, heading for the beach below. Carrick paused, and suddenly strangely, his quarry stopped, turned, and seemed to be looking straight up towards him.

Then Carrick heard the snap of a twig behind him, started to swing round, and felt something hard explode against the side of his head.

The next thing he was vaguely aware of was that he was lying on the path, that a figure bent over him and that he heard a chuckle. The figure stepped away, gave a soft, two-note whistle which was some kind of signal, then more pebbles rattled.

At least another minute passed before he had strength enough to struggle upright again. Head throbbing still dazed, he looked down the dark slope again. All he could see was the faint outline of the rocks beside the shore and the white line of surf where the waves broke against them.

He gave up and made a weary, stumbling return to Fean House. On the way, a rabbit scurried in front of him, stopped, then scampered off again. He was glad it hadn't stopped to fight – the way he felt, the rabbit might have won.

'Two of them,' said Captain James Shannon a few minutes later with minimal satisfaction and considerable sarcasm. 'Well, at least you found out something.'

'It always helps,' said Carrick defensively.

He was sitting in a chair in a downstairs room at Fean House, clutching a cloth soaked in cold water against the aching bruise on the side of his head, holding a glass of whisky in his other hand, and the whisky seemed the more effective of the two.

Shannon was standing over him, scowling in frustration. Across the room, Dorothy Vullan sat on a couch smoking a cigarette while Shona bandaged the graze on her arm. The room curtains were tightly closed, Shannon had moved the chairs clear of the window, and Milne Vullan was prowling in the background nursing an old deer-stalking rifle.

'Milne, put that thing down,' said the Witch of the Isles wearily. 'All you're doing is making me nervous. Anyway if they stuck to that path they've gone now – probably the same way they came.'

Shona Grant stopped bandaging, looked puzzled, then nodded agreement.

'It would take them to the north end of the island,' she said soberly. 'The tide is out. They could make it on foot back to the mainland, if they didn't mind wading a couple of stretches.'

'You're right.' Vullan sighed and dumped the rifle on a vacant chair. 'Well, I've phoned John Marsh at the cottage. He's coming over.'

'Does anyone else live on the island?' asked Carrick.

'No.'

'Tradition,' said Dorothy Vullan unemotionally, drawing on her cigarette. 'Even the ones who work here prefer to get home before dark.' Her mouth tightened. 'These two who came over must have felt quite brave.'

Shannon grunted. 'They didn't mean to do more than scare you – this time, anyway.'

'Firing a shotgun at that range?' protested Shona.

'At that range he couldn't miss unless he wanted to,' said Shannon in a cold, factual voice. He put a hand in his jacket pocket, drew it out again, but kept his fingers closed around whatever he was holding. 'I took a look outside, where the shotgun pellets should have hit the stonework. Here's what I found.'

His hand flicked and three small, twisted, blackened silver coins rattled on the low coffee table in front of Dorothy Vullan. She leaned forward, stared at them, then carefully stubbed out her cigarette, green eyes showing neither anger nor fear but something close to disbelief.

'You know what they are, Captain?' she asked softly. 'And why?'

Shannon nodded.

'Old-fashioned silver sixpences.' She gave a small, tight laugh. 'There is only one way you can shoot a witch. You should load the gun with a silver bullet – but a crooked silver sixpence will do.'

'What kind of sick mind plays a fool trick like this?' asked Milne Vullan hoarsely.

Shannon didn't answer. There was a knock at the front door and Vullan hesitated, then picked up the rifle again and went out of the room. A moment later they heard him talking to Marsh in the hallway.

'I didn't think I'd ever be glad John Marsh was around,' said Dorothy Vullan with a grimace, listening. 'He tries, but we don't get on. Still –' She paused, looked again at the blackened, twisted little coins, and shook her head. 'Malicious, superstitious gossip – and it leads to this. Can you understand it, Chief Officer?'

Carrick hesitated. Shona Grant had come close beside the Witch of the Isles and had a hand on her shoulder. Face wiped of expression, Shannon obviously wasn't going to give him any help.

'I know plenty of city people who won't walk under ladders, and not just because something might fall on their heads.' Carrick finished his drink in a gulp while choosing the rest of his words. 'The fishing crews don't totally understand what your husband is doing.'

'But his wife is the Witch of the Isles, and that's enough?' she suggested resignedly.

'For a few of them,' agreed Carrick. 'Particularly if other things they don't understand start happening, if it begins to look as though it is dangerous to quarrel with the Witch.'

'George MacKenzie.' The village constable's name came from her lips like a sigh.

'But they can't blame you,' protested Shona. 'He had an accident, he drowned –'

'Somebody broke an arm, somebody else's car crashed' – Dorothy Vullan grimaced – 'people remember things, Shona. I'm probably being blamed for what happened to your father's boat.'

'What was your quarrel with MacKenzie?' asked Shannon.

'A stupid thing. A few months ago the office at the seaweed plant was vandalized by a couple of juveniles from the village. MacKenzie didn't do anything about it because he knew their parents – and I complained to the Chief Constable, who had him on the carpet.' She shrugged. 'It just grew from there.'

Shannon gave a stifled grunt then left it at that as Marsh and Vullan came into the room. Marsh was wearing a duffel coat over old slacks and a sweater and went straight to Dorothy Vullan.

'I was halfway to bed when Milne called,' he said, with a concerned frown at the bandage on her arm. 'You're all right?'

'I'll survive,' she said dryly, lighting a fresh cigarette.

'Good.' Chewing his lip, he faced Shannon and Carrick. 'Milne is worried about calling in the police. I'm – well inclined to agree with him.'

Shannon raised a surprised eyebrow.

'I overheard some of what Carrick said,' Vullan told him, and shifted his feet awkwardly. 'If this has anything to do with the fishing trials, they've almost completed. I – yes, I only need another couple of days at most.' He paused hopefully. 'Once they've stopped, maybe that'll finish any trouble. But it might make things even worse if the police were tramping around.'

'It's worth trying,' said Dorothy Vullan slowly. 'Captain?'

'One of my officers was attacked,' said Shannon bleakly. 'It's just lucky he has a thick skull. But if that's what you want –' He stopped there and shrugged.

John Marsh elected to stay at Fean House for the rest of the night and there was no opposition from the Vullans. A little later Milne Vullan and his rifle escorted Shannon, Carrick and Shona Grant down to the jetty and as the patrol launch creamed away from the island they caught a last glimpse of him, a tall, sombre figure standing in the darkness with Fean House silhouetted above against the night sky.

Shannon had the helm, and hardly spoke until he had steered across the channel and they were back inside the Feanport breakwater. Then, as he throttled back and crawled the launch past the black shapes of the moored fishing fleet, heading towards *Marlin*'s berth, he gave a familiar throat-clearing noise.

'I'll land you two first, mister,' he told Carrick. 'We can talk in the morning. But it'll be an early start – we've those damned voting papers to deliver around the islands, and the sooner that's done the better.' He scowled till his beard curled. 'We'll treat it as a dummy run for the ballet-box collections – and that's going to be done fast.'

Moments later, he let the launch drift alongside a flight of stone steps that led up to the quay. Carrick and Shona stepped out, Shannon growled a good night, and the launch murmured along towards *Marlin,* where an eagle-eyed petty officer was already waiting with some deck hands to hoist it back aboard.

Feanport's inhabitants were mainly early to bed, early to rise people. Only a few lights showed in the village and the harbour was deserted as Carrick and Shona Grant walked the length of the quay past the silent lines of fishing boats.

Outside the harbour, she turned to the right along a pathway which stayed close to the shore. Carrick took her hand and she smiled at him as her fingers laced in his. Then they walked on, listening to countless, unseen seabirds piping and crying in the darkness, feeding along the tideline. For a background, there was the steady, rhythmic wash of the sea and the murmur of a solitary fishing boat coming in.

The beacon lights on the breakwater were there to guide it. Out across the water, another glint of light marked Fean House. Slowing, Shona Grant looked towards the glint.

'I wish –' she began, then stopped and faced him. 'No, I'm not going to talk about it. Not right now.'

'Good.' Quietly, Carrick brought her close to him and their lips met. For a moment, he felt the warmth of her body against his own and she pressed against him while they kissed again. Then she smiled, stood back, still holding his hand.

'I've an old-fashioned father waiting at home,' she said. 'He's already peeved enough about where I've been.'

'There's tomorrow,' said Carrick hopefully. 'I can fix the evening ashore if –'

She nodded and looked pleased. 'I'd like that. Collect me from the cottage?'

'If it's still safe,' he said wryly. 'Is there any place we could go for a meal?'

'The nearest is well outside Feanport,' she admitted. 'But I can borrow a car.' She paused and looked at him thoughtfully. 'Webb, how long will *Marlin* be here?'

'Today is Tuesday, the election is Thursday.' He gave a resigned shrug. 'We'll probably resume patrol on Friday, unless –' He stopped it there.

'Unless there's more trouble?' she asked quietly, glancing out across the water towards the dark shape of Fean Island.

Carrick nodded. 'You've known them a long time, haven't you?'

'Yes.' Then she surprised him. 'Dorothy Vullan and my mother were cousins.'

They began walking along the path again, slowly.

'Then it's a family quarrel,' said Carrick, frowning. 'I knew it went far back, but –'

'My mother died soon after I was born,' said Shona unemotionally. 'Dorothy and Milne wanted to adopt me – they knew by then they couldn't have children. My father said no, they persisted, he told them to go to hell – and it smouldered on that way. He didn't involve me in it, and I could visit them all I wanted. But he'd have nothing to do with them.' She shook her head. 'They even helped pay my way through university when I left Feanport and he knew it – but he'll never admit it.'

'But you didn't come back to Feanport,' mused Carrick. 'He's proud of the job you've got with Anglo-Norge. How do you feel about it?'

'Being part of the oil game?' She chewed her lip for a moment. 'It's the same for most girls who grow up in Feanport. Either you marry a fisherman, or you leave the place – there's not much else. I move around with Anglo-Norge, I work on their North Sea production forward planning team, I like it – and they pay well. But sometimes I still miss what's here.'

They kept on along the path for another moment or two in silence, the sea and the piping terns a tranquil background. Ahead of them, almost at the end of the village, a small cottage sat a little way back from the path with a light burning above the porch.

'I knew it,' she said with an affectionate irritation. 'He's waiting.' Then her manner changed. 'Webb, I'm worried about what's going on. Mainly because I can't understand it. Whatever else my father said about Dorothy Vullan, he always scoffed at this Witch of the Isles business. But now –'

'Does he go along with it?'

'He'll take anyone's side against her.' Shona's fingers tightened against Carrick's as she spoke. 'Even the way those damned fool MacLeans, all three of them, are blaming her for that gas cylinder exploding on the *Rachel* – he doesn't stop them.'

'How many others maybe feel the same way?' asked Carrick bluntly.

'A few,' she shrugged. 'Not many, but enough to make trouble.'

'The MacLeans have their own problems,' he mused. 'Lachie was in a small punch-up in the village tonight. Three men jumped him – he says he doesn't know who they were, or why.'

She winced. 'I didn't know.'

They had almost reached the cottage. Looking at the light shining above the porch again, Shona hesitated then glanced at Carrick apologetically.

'I won't ask you in,' she told him. 'I – well, I think I'd better tell him myself what happened over there.'

Carrick nodded his understanding, released her hand, then had a thought.

'Help me with one thing,' he said slowly. 'There's a little man with an eye-patch I've seen around the harbour. He was talking to your father. Do you know him?'

'That's Lampeye.' Her grey eyes showed a slight surprise at the question. 'Harry Duggan, but everybody calls him Lampeye. He used to crew on the *Rachel*.'

'Till?'

'Till he came aboard drunk once too often,' Shona frowned a little. 'Now he sometimes helps Milne Vullan on the *Sea Whip*. Poor old Lampeye – he was the last of the old crew on the *Rachel*.'

'Then the MacLeans moved in?' Carrick felt puzzled. 'When did that happen?'

'Three or four months ago. At least, that's when Donnie and Willie moved in. Cousin Lachie arrived a little later, after Lampeye got the boot.' She shrugged. 'They work well, even though they're not Feanport men.'

'Outsiders?' queried Carrick.

She laughed. 'From Stornoway – around here, you're a foreigner if you can't go back ten generations among the headstones in the churchyard.' She paused and glanced towards the cottage. 'Webb, I'll bet that father of mine is watching round the edge of a curtain. So – good night.'

She had gone before he could answer. Carrick waited until she'd opened the cottage door which, West Highland style, wasn't locked, and probably hadn't been for years. Then, hands in his pockets, he headed back along the shoreside path. Shona Grant was occupying a lot of his thoughts, but not all of them – and his destination wasn't the harbour.

Two men had been involved in the shotgun episode at Fean Island. Donnie MacLean and his cousin Lachie were gradually strengthening as possible candidates and it would do no harm to see if they were home.

Five minutes' brisk walking took him through the streets of the sleeping village to the little cottage with the rowan branch above the door. The front of the cottage was in darkness but he circled round the small patch of garden, cursing under his breath as his clothes snagged an unseen thorn bush, then stopped as he saw a chink of light showing at one of the rear windows.

The only sound he could hear was the low murmur of the wind yet for a moment he looked around with a vague, uneasy feeling that he wasn't alone. Something moved in a patch of shadow, he tensed, then relaxed again as a small owl rose and flapped silently away with the limp body of a vole in its claws.

Grinning, relieved, he crossed to the window on tiptoe, pressed his nose against the glass, and looked round the edge of a piece of ragged curtaining into the kitchen of the cottage.

Both MacLeans were in the room, eating in their shirt-sleeves at the kitchen table. As he watched, Donnie MacLean rose, took his plate over towards a trash bucket, scraped what was left of his meal into the bucket, and dumped the plate into the nearby sink. When he came back to the table he brought two cans of beer with him and dumped one in front of Lachie MacLean.

The two men grinned, Lachie MacLean said something in a low voice which made his cousin laugh, then they raised the cans in a toast of some kind before they drank. But something else in the room interested Carrick more than the MacLeans' eating habits. The inevitable peat fire was smouldering in the kitchen's old-fashioned fireplace and laid out to dry on the hearth in front of it, visibly steaming, was a jumble of damp clothing.

Dorothy Vullan had said anyone could cross on foot to the north end of the island from the mainland at low tide, if they didn't mind wading a couple of stretches – having seen enough, Carrick drew back.

He was easing round to the front of the cottage again when a rustle of sound reached his ears. It came from almost the same place as before, but this time it was no owl.

Without giving any indication of haste, he altered his

route so that he skirted a patch of gorse bush. Then, at the last minute, he pounced round the side of the bush on the figure who was crouching there. He heard a low yelp of fear but the figure didn't even try to struggle – and he found himself face to face with the little man with the eye-patch.

'Out of there,' said Carrick softly, shifting his grip to the neck of the cringing Lampeye's thick wool sweater. 'Move.'

Trembling but silent, the little man allowed himself to be dragged several yards away from the cottage till they were behind what looked like a toolshed. Carrick stopped him there.

'Following me again?' he asked icily. 'That's getting to be a habit with you.'

'I wasn't – honest, I wasn't.' Lampeye had a piping voice, accentuated by a note of panic, and there was liquor on his breath.

'Don't try to tell me you were meditating under that bush,' said Carrick and shook his head. 'You're not the type, Lampeye. You're just a nasty little nuisance.'

'I came after you earlier, right,' said the little man with a quivering earnestness. 'I – well, I was curious, that's all.' He swallowed and straightened his narrow shoulders with an attempt at dignity. 'An' it's not my fault you came along an' started snooping at the MacLeans' window. I was there first, followed them all the way from the harbour –'

'When?' Startled, Carrick eased his grip a little.

'About an hour back.' Lampeye's one good eye blinked at him in sudden, faint moonlight as the clouds overhead thinned for a moment. 'But they didn't come off a boat, more likely from the north shore.'

'All right.' Carrick drew a deep breath. 'You followed them to the cottage. After that, why hang around behind that bush?'

The little man scowled and shrugged, saying nothing.

'Try,' suggested Carrick softly. 'Otherwise, I'll march you back to the MacLeans, heave you in their door, and tell them where I caught you – your word against mine.'

'No, don't.' Lampeye quivered at the thought. 'Look, it was the way they went sneakin' along, like they didn't want anyone to see them. Their clothes were wet, drippin' wet, as if they'd been swimming in them. I stayed because I wondered what the hell they'd been up to, that's all.'

'Was either of them carrying anything?' asked Carrick. The question drew only a puzzled headshake and he'd expected that. If the MacLeans had been the shotgun heroes, they wouldn't want to risk advertising it. The gun could be hidden anywhere from a rabbit hole onward. 'Tell me something different, Lampeye. Angus Grant fired you from the *Rachel* for being drunk, correct?'

'I'd had a drink, but I wasn't drunk,' protested Lampeye in a shrill indignation then gulped and lowered his voice again as Carrick glared. 'The skipper just wanted rid o' me, to make room for the last o' those damned MacLeans. He wanted younger hands, thought he'd get more work out o' them.'

'That's life,' said Carrick dryly. 'How big a grudge does that leave you holding?'

'Me?' Lampeye inched closer, his stale breath unpleasantly near, and moistened his lips. 'Well, I'll tell you –'

Suddenly, unexpectedly, he kicked Carrick hard on the shin. The pain was enough to loosen Carrick's grip on the wool sweater for an instant, and an instant was enough for the little man to wrench free and start running.

Swearing, Carrick stayed where he was and ruefully rubbed his leg. Lampeye had already disappeared among the cottages and he had a feeling the little man would prove very hard to find again. Sighing, he caught himself reaching for the non-existent cigarettes in his pocket, remembered, swore sadly this time, and, still limping a little, started walking back towards the harbour and *Marlin*.

Whatever else might happen that night, he'd had enough.

The snow which had threatened began falling for a spell just before dawn. It came lightly and briefly, just enough to leave a dusting of white on the hills above Feanport and a thin coating of puddled slush around the wakening harbour area, then the sky cleared.

Marlin sailed as the sun came up. A lively, spume-laced sea was waiting outside the shelter of the bay and she was soon thrusting a dipping, heaving way, spray drenching along her length, while a gusting, chilling north-east wind clawed at her flag and sang through her aerial rigging. Decks vibrating as the big twin diesels drove her on, the slim grey shape swung west and quickly left the mainland astern.

Webb Carrick had the watch but Shannon was in the command chair with a full bridge team around him, a planned schedule as tight and complex as a railway timetable ahead, and a crew who knew he was determined to keep to it for his own personal satisfaction. In the chartroom, Ferguson was in charge of a pile of sealed black metal ballot boxes and carefully labelled bundles of voting papers. Jumbo Wills and Clapper Bell had a boat's crew huddled ready in the shelter of a deck house aft and any man aboard who had a hangover knew the best thing to do was keep quiet about it.

The first of the six islands on the delivery run appeared ahead exactly an hour after *Marlin* had cleared Feanport. An isolated dot on the radar screen became a green hump of land, a scatter of houses and a man with a horse waiting on a white strip of shell-sand beach.

Using the bridge glasses, Captain Shannon watched impatiently while the fishery cruiser's boat tossed through the surf to land the first of the ballot boxes and voting papers. The transfer was made, the horseman waved farewell, and as soon as the boat was back aboard *Marlin* got under way again.

At the next island it was the same, except that there was a small stone quay where an old van and a young driver were waiting. Then the fishery cruiser turned on a new, south-west course for almost another hour through the lumping seas till it came in under the lee of a spectacular sea-bird cliff of black volcanic basalt.

The transfer there was made by rocket line while screaming hordes of disturbed gulls and terns wheeled overhead. The island was called Harvaig, eighteen adults and four children lived there, and in winter even small boats could only land on it about once a month, when tide and weather were exactly right.

As a rehearsal for the Thursday night collection run, Harvaig was the furthest west and most difficult of the six islands to be visited. *Marlin*'s wake curved south as she left, and Shannon ticked off one more point on the mental pattern of geometic lines he had decided on to cover the fishery cruiser's task in minimum sailing time.

They passed other islands and saw many more on the radar screen – but they were empty, inhabited at most by a few winter-grazing sheep.

It had been different once. Ruined steadings, abandoned villages, occasional tumbledown castles told an earlier story. But of the five hundred islands in the long Hebridean chain only about a hundred were now populated and of that hundred only seven could boast a population of over two thousand. Beauty was one thing. Harsh economic reality had left only those isolated handfuls of people while the descendants of earlier emigrant generations were scattered far across the world.

The delivery run kept on. The fourth island, the largest, had almost a hundred inhabitants and a long, modern pier – built by the navy for wartime use, now home for a couple of forty-foot-long line boats. That left two tiny communities of lighthouse keepers and crofters, where the ballet boxes were landed by boat again.

It was noon, they had been at sea for a shade over four hours, and only the straight run back to Feanport remained. As if in agreement, the weather began moderating and the fishery cruiser's pitching roll settled to a regular vibration. Captain Shannon retired to his day cabin to go over his calculations again and the atmosphere on the bridge immediately relaxed. Ferguson disappeared and a little later Jumbo Wills arrived to take over the watch.

As soon as he'd been relieved Carrick left the bridge and went down to his cabin. He shaved for the first time that day, tapped the pack of cigarettes taped to the mirror as if it was a barometer, then went along to the wardroom.

The lunch menu was cod steak and a tasteless pudding but he was hungry. Andy Shaw, the chief engineer, was there too, ate with him, then dragged out his cigarettes as he finished.

'Still off them?' queried Shaw sardonically. He grinned at Carrick's nod, lit a cigarette, flicked the used match into the emptied coffee cup in front of him, and sat back. 'I had the Old Man round my neck again about the *Rachel* – soon as he got back from that bunfight last night.'

'Saying what?' Carrick watched the smoke rise from the cigarette with a stony face.

'Saying nothing, just asking the same questions he did before,' complained Shaw. 'But how the hell do I know what happened when anything you might call evidence had vanished – cylinder, feed pipe, the lot? Laddie, I'm just a simple engineer.'

Simple engineers were a bloody-minded race apart, decided Carrick. But there was another approach that sometimes worked with Shaw.

'I suppose it would need a fair amount of skill to rig an

explosion,' he mused. 'But suppose we were talking about an engineer, someone who had that kind of skill?'

'Skill?' Shaw gave a caustic grunt. 'The way I'd have done it would have blown the whole backside off that boat. No, from the looks of things this was different. Amateur style and –' He stopped, eyes narrowing, and swore softly. 'Conned me again, haven't you?'

'Well?' invited Carrick dryly. 'What's amateur style?'

'A couple of minutes aboard and a half-turn or so with a shift key,' said Shaw wearily. 'That way, you'd get a pin-sized leak of gas that would take time to build up. But eventually you'd have a pool of gas waiting, and the smell wouldn't be noticed in the stink aboard the average fishing boat. Then if someone went below and struck a match to light that stove – wham.'

'And the cylinder?'

'Depends,' shrugged Shaw. 'It could have been just the freed gas, maybe the cylinder didn't explode at all.' He scowled and rose. 'But I deal in facts, remember – I leave guesswork where it belongs, on deck.'

Grinning, Carrick watched him go then poured himself another cup of coffee and sipped it slowly. The chief engineer's theory made sense. But put it against the way in which any evidence had vanished and the whole situation went straight back into the melting pot.

He was still thinking about it a little later, when he made his way back up to the bridge. Captain Shannon was back in the command chair, Jumbo Wills had been relegated to a stance beside the radar screen, and a v.h.f. feed from the radio room was muttering away on the bulkhead-mounted loudspeaker.

Hanging back for a moment, he looked around. *Marlin* was still on schedule for the run and they were back in the Brannan Sound, on the approach towards Feanport again. The distinctive mainland bulk of Broch Point was to starboard. Over to port, about half a mile away, lay the flat, glistening shape of the Witchrock.

Shannon saw him and beckoned him over.

'Nicely timed, mister,' he declared with a caustic relief which seemed aimed at Jumbo Wills. 'We've company about a mile ahead – Feanport boats. Tell me what you make of them. Mister Wills hasn't any helpful ideas.'

Sheepishly, Jumbo Wills handed Carrick the bridge glasses. Standing in a stiff-shouldered way, the duty helmsman seemed to be trying to pretend he didn't exist. Wondering what was going on, Carrick focussed the glasses on two broad-beamed, dark-hulled motor fishing vessels. They were travelling very slowly, about fifty yards apart, their trawl warps visible and running taut into the water at an odd angle astern. Figures were running back and forward on their decks, a small cloud of seabirds circled low overhead, and he took a guess at the rest.

'Pair-trawling,' he suggested, putting down the glasses. That part was easy enough – pair-trawling, two boats operating a single net, was a reasonably common way of fishing. 'They're trying to haul it in – but it looks like they've caught themselves a problem.'

'It sounds like it too,' grunted Shannon, thumbing towards the loudspeaker. 'They've asked for another boat to come out and lend a hand.' He leaned forward. 'Helmsman, alter course – steer fine towards them. Mr Wills, let's not make it look like a cavalry charge.'

Crossing to the telegraph control, Wills managed a grimace in Carrick's direction and raised his eyes to heaven in silent appeal.

It was an almost unbelievable scene that met their eyes minutes later. *Marlin* had come alongside the pair-trawl boats and lay about a ship's length distant, her diesels lazily holding steerage way – and over there, between the boats, the great net bag of their trawl showed hauled almost to the surface.

Swollen and bulging, it held a close-packed struggling mass of fish of every kind. Wriggling silver and brown shapes frothed the surface of the blue-green swell in a frenzy amid the constant raucous excitement of the circling gulls overhead.

'What a jackpot,' said Jumbo Wills in an almost bemused voice, staring from the bridge wing. 'If they get that lot ashore –'

'That's their problem,' said Captain Shannon sardonically, elbowing a way between Wills and Carrick with a battery-powered loudhailer in his hands. 'Too big a catch, and they can't haul it in.'

Life seethed within the net's confines – cod and coalfish, grey mullet and spotted dogfish struggled and thrashed with a score of other species. There were larger shapes there too, a giant skate that easily topped the two-hundred-pound mark and a young blue shark among them.

'So what'll they do, sir?' asked Wills, puzzled. 'Let some of them go, or –'

'Throw away money?' Shannon shook his head, raised the loudhailer to his lips, and his voice boomed metallically across the water. 'Captain Shannon, Fishery Protection – can we assist?'

A figure wearing overalls and a green tam o' shanter had emerged from the wheelhouse of the nearest boat carrying a hailer.

'No need, but thank you,' he bellowed back. 'We've burned out a winch, that's all. There's another boat on the way now – we'll brail some o' the catch, then cope with the rest.'

Brailing meant the third boat would come in with a small scoop net and remove some of the weight from the overloaded trawl bag. Looking down at the two bobbing fishing boats and the burden straining their trawl warps, Carrick knew it was about the only course open to them.

Pair-trawlers worked with one main legal limitation – the trawl they dragged between them mustn't touch the seabed. But once the trawl had been 'shot' then the arc between them gradually tightened and normally both ends were transferred to the one boat to haul in. With a catch like this one they'd been in trouble from the start. One boat couldn't have handled it, and an overstrained winch packing in completed their predicament.

Shannon wasn't finished. Leaning his elbows on the rail, a glint in his eyes, he used the loudhailer again.

'You're in the money, skipper,' he congratulated through the rasping amplifier. 'Ever had a run like this in the Brannan Sound before?'

The figure in the tam o' shanter didn't answer for a moment, then they saw him shrug.

'Sometimes you're lucky, Captain,' came his bellowed reply. 'We had a hunch, that's all. No need to stand by us – we'll be fine.'

Carefully, Shannon switched off his loudhailer, waved an acknowledgement, and scowled at Carrick.

'Luck and a hunch,' he snapped sarcastically. 'Damned liars, Mr Wills –'

'Sir?' Jumbo Wills blinked.

'Resume course and speed. Log the sighting and their registration numbers.' Going into the bridge, he dumped the loudhailer on a signal locker, then beckoned Carrick. 'Come with me.'

The fishery cruiser was already getting under way again as Carrick followed him into the cramped space of the chartroom. Grunting under his breath, Shannon dragged out a large-scale Admiralty chart of the Brannan Sound and spread it on the table.

'You know what I'm thinking, mister?' he demanded.

'Fish-herding – Milne Vullan's way,' said Carrick quietly.

'He told us he only needed a few more days.' Shannon frowned at the chart then gave a satisfied nod. 'Yes, and those two were pair-trawling north. Take a look and see how you read it.'

It took a few moments study of the chart before Carrick understood, then it suddenly became clear. The chart's depth readings showed an average of thirty fathoms of water in most of the Brannan Sound. But there was an exception, a deep, narrow undersea valley of eighty fathoms marked as running slightly west of centre from near Fean Bay all the way south until it reached the Witch-rock, which sat like a marker where the valley widened out.

'If he used this electrical system from the *Sea Whip* somewhere north of us, in this trough –' Carrick ran his finger down the chart, paused, and raised an eyebrow at Shannon.

'Add two skippers who would help and keep their mouths shut,' nodded Shannon. 'He'd start the fish running south, down the trough – most of them would prefer to stay in deep water. That trawl net would be sitting waiting like a cork in a bottle.'

'Then where is he?' posed Carrick, puzzled.

'How the hell should I know?' snarled Shannon and scowled out of the chartroom window. The two fishing boats had vanished astern and the fishery cruiser was cutting her way through the swell at a steady, thrusting pace. 'He's probably back home at Fean Island by now – the skippers can tell him all he wants later.'

'And they'll tell him that his fish-herding worked,' mused Carrick. 'If that's a sample of what he can do –'

'Then it's not fishing,' said Shannon bleakly, cutting him short. 'It's the next best thing to vacuum cleaning the sea, mister. And I'm old-fashioned enough to think that's a damned sight worse than witchcraft.'

CHAPTER FIVE

A faint dusting of snow still whitened the hills above Feanport as *Marlin* returned to harbour and eased back into her berth at the south quay. Milne Vullan's *Sea Whip* was moored further along, empty and deserted, and there was one new arrival among the other craft in harbour. The twice-weekly mailboat from the Outer Isles, making its inward run from Stornoway, had tied up at the north quay and a small squad of dock workers were unloading an assortment of cargo from her holds.

Webb Carrick went ashore almost as soon as the fishery cruiser's gangway had been run out. He took Clapper Bell with him, and a brief talk session in the scuba compartment beforehand had brought *Marlin*'s bo'sun up-to-date with the main outline of the puzzle hanging over the Brannan Sound. Now, with Captain Shannon's wary blessing, the first call on their list was to be the harbourmaster's office.

An extra ingredient had been added to Feanport's usual atmosphere while they'd been away. With less than a day remaining until the election booths opened, some of the political parties seemed to have decided to make at least a token attempt at wooing the fishing village's voters. Two sound trucks were braying slogans and tape-recorded messages at the harbour gates, trying hard to compete against each other and the steady rumble of the quayside crane working at the mailboat.

'Noisy sods,' said Clapper Bell dourly, ambling along beside Carrick. 'That's two who wouldn't get my vote.'

Carrick grinned. 'It's called involvement, Clapper. Back your choice and hope you've picked a winner.'

'Not me.' Bell kicked an old fish head which was lying among the litter on the quayside. As it flew, a gull swooped and snatched it up. 'Any time I vote, it's to keep somebody out, not to put anyone in.'

The sound trucks were still duelling as they entered the harbourmaster's office, a small single-storey brick building with a flagstaff that needed a coat of paint and a noticeboard that looked ready to crumble away with age. Inside, they found Shuggy Morrison seated beside a glow-ing anthracite stove with a mug of tea on one hand and a tattered comic book in the other. Behind him, a v.h.f. receiver murmured away, tuned to the fishing waveband.

'You two.' The elderly, red-faced harbourmaster gave them an uneasy nod, set down the comic book, and stayed seated. 'What do you want this time? I thought I told you last night –'

'That you keep your nose clean,' agreed Carrick wearily. He considered the shabbily dressed figure and shook his head. 'You've got a comfortable number here, Shuggy. It's a shame to spoil it.'

'Eh?' Morrison heaved to his feet, alarmed, tea slopping from his mug. 'Meaning what?'

'You might have a problem,' said Carrick sadly. 'For instance, if Fishery Protection made complaining noises to the harbour trustees about you. Nothing specific, just noises –'

'I've seen it happen,' said Clapper Bell sympathetically. He picked up the discarded comic book and glanced at its pages. 'Then your bosses move in. Checkin' your paperwork. Awkward questions about things like whether any skipper ever hands you a present for favours. They'd want everything tightened up, smartened up – hell, they'd maybe even make you wear a clean shirt every day.'

'All that because you didn't want to help,' mused Carrick. 'Yes, it's hard luck.'

Morrison swallowed, stared at them for a moment, then capitulated with a groan.

'So what is it this time?' he asked warily.

'Friendly co-operation.' Carrick exchanged a solemn nod with Clapper Bell. 'Let's start with Vullan's *Sea Whip*. How long since it came in?'

'Half an hour maybe,' shrugged Morrison. 'He brought his wife an' John Marsh over from the island. If you want him, try the village hall – he's fixin' up things for the voting tomorrow.' He saw Carrick's raised eyebrow and added hastily, 'He looked in wi' a message for me to pass on to one o' the mailboat passengers when she docked.'

'Tell,' said Clapper Bell, flicking over a page of the comic book, not looking up.

'His name is Chester – he's here to see Dorothy Vullan.' The harbourmaster took a gloomy swallow of tea. 'You just missed him.'

'Ever seen him before?' asked Carrick then, as Morrison

shook his head, flicked a thumb towards the radio. 'Two of the local boats have a problem. You heard?'

'Caught too much fish.' Morrison managed a lopsided grin. 'They made enough noise about it.'

'Are the skippers friends of Milne Vullan?'

'Maybe not friends –' began Morrison.

'That's a hell o' an answer,' sighed Clapper Bell, his voice a masterpiece of solicitude. 'I'm sorry for you, Shuggy.'

'What I mean is they – well, they maybe help him out,' wheezed Morrison hastily. 'The word is the Witch of the Isles puts a good catch their way to square the bill.'

'Then I want to know next time they're doing it,' said Carrick grimly. 'These two, or any other boat going out for that kind of reason. You get word to me on *Marlin* the moment you hear.'

'I'll try.' Morrison spread his podgy, broken-nailed hands in resignation. 'I can't guarantee it.'

Carrick turned his back on the man and went over to the grimy window, looking out at the harbour scene. One of the sound trucks had driven off, the crew of the other seemed to be having a coffee break.

'Seen anything of Angus Grant or the MacLeans this morning?' he asked suddenly.

'They were around.' Morrison gave a woebegone nod. 'Willie MacLean is out o' the hospital, bandaged like a mummy but healthy enough.'

'Three men had a try at beating up Lachie MacLean last night.' Carrick paused and looked round. 'He claims he doesn't know them, or why. But I met a little man called Lampeye –

'Him?' Morrison snorted at the thought. 'Lampeye isn't the physical type – even when he's drunk. He talks, but I know his style. More likely he'd –' he stopped short, as if regretting what he'd almost said.

'More likely he'd do a sabotage job on the *Rachel* or release a truck handbrake?' suggested Carrick. He saw he wasn't going to get an answer and switched back again. 'All right, but there were three men and they were set to give Lachie MacLean a hammering.'

'I haven't heard,' said the harbourmaster uneasily.

'But?'

The man shrugged. 'There's Archie Campbell, another o' Angus Grant's old crew. He works at a garage in the village now – and he's big enough and thick enough to fight anyone. He doesn't talk much, but he has as big a grudge against the MacLeans as Lampeye.' He licked his lips, suddenly aghast. 'Look, I didn't tell you that –'

'You didn't say a word,' murmured Carrick. 'Just remember, if any boat leaves here to help the *Sea Whip* you get word to us.'

'Fast,' said Clapper Bell cheerfully, and tossed down the comic book. 'Thanks, Shuggy. I'll come back and finish the story – find out if the girl ever gets her clothes back on.'

'Don't hurry,' said Morrison bitterly, and turned away to brew himself a new mug of tea,

Outside the office, the remaining sound truck was producing metallic throat-clearing noises. A girl member of its team, wearing tight jeans and a sweater, seemed to be making non-political progress with a couple of admiring fishermen. Clapper Bell threw an appraising look in her direction, then glanced at Carrick.

'Want me to find Campbell?' he asked bluntly.

Carrick nodded. 'Try him. Then ask around about the MacLeans – how other people feel about them. But don't make too many waves, Clapper. Not yet.'

They parted, the big Glasgow-Irishman taking a route which took him closely past the girl at the sound truck, Carrick heading up the climbing road which led to the village.

When he reached the hall the main door was lying open and a couple of workmen were erecting screens for a set of polling booths inside. Further back, Milne Vullan was standing talking to an elderly woman, who was spreading papers on a table top. Vullan saw him, exchanged a final smiling word with the woman, then came over.

'Decisions, decisions,' he murmured dryly. 'She wants a screen in front of the table, so men won't look at her legs. At her age, that's being hopeful.' He paused, stuck his hands in his pockets, and asked, 'How did the delivery run go?'

'On schedule.' Carrick shrugged that part of the morning aside. 'We met a couple of boats pair-netting on the way back – they'd hit a jackpot.' He raised an eyebrow. 'Or maybe you knew?'

'Let's say I'll be talking to them later,' temporized Vullan easily. 'I told you, Webb – I only need a little more time and believe me, after last night I'm being careful.'

'No more visitors?'

Vullan shook his head, looked past him, and brightened. 'Not the way you mean. But there's someone I'd like you to meet.'

He led Carrick further up the hall to where Dorothy Vullan and a stranger stood looking up at a stained glass window. The Witch of the Isles wore slacks and a white rollneck sweater, an outfit which only emphasized her striking looks and personality. The stranger, a tall, thin, sandy-haired man in a dark sports suit, laughed at something she said then the conversation ended as Vullan and Carrick arrived.

'Meet Robert Chester,' introduced Vullan. 'A wandering Englishman – he came in on the mailboat.'

Chester smiled and gave Carrick a firm handshake as the introductions were completed. He had strong white teeth and boyish good looks and at a guess Carrick placed him in his late thirties.

'Robert is in the antiques game,' said Dorothy Vullan dryly. 'That's how we met. He's up from London on another of what he calls his re-stocking trips – which means a plundering expedition.'

'I'm the one who feels plundered,' said Chester lazily. 'They drive a damned hard bargain among the islands.'

Milne Vullan grinned unsympathetically. 'You'll still show a profit. How much did you buy this time?'

'A little here, a little there,' shrugged Chester. 'I've five crates being unloaded from the mailboat to be sent south by road. Though' – he glanced significantly at Dorothy Vullan – 'I'm still open for business.'

'No,' she said firmly, then ran a hand over her copper-bronze hair and chuckled. 'We'll still give you lunch. But any bits and pieces at Fean House stay there – you've been told that before.'

'So I keep trying.' The sandy-haired man shrugged at Carrick. 'She has some Jacobean glass I'm after, but she's stubborn.'

'They're all stubborn,' said Carrick fervently. 'Staying long?'

Chester shook his head. 'Just long enough to check those crates. I'll be driving south before dusk.'

'Then we'd better get you across to the island,' declared Milne Vullan and frowned around the hall. 'Where the hell has Lampeye gone?'

'He vanished out the back door when Fishery Protection appeared on the scene,' said Dorothy Vullan. She eyed Carrick with unconcealed curiosity. 'I'm not sure why.'

'We've some unfinished business,' said Carrick dryly. The little one-eyed fisherman was obviously going to prove difficult to pin down. 'You can tell him I haven't forgotten.'

'It's – well, nothing to do with last night, is it?' Milne Vullan was frankly incredulous. 'I mean, that would be crazy. Lampeye's harmless – and he spends half his time helping me on the *Sea Whip*.'

'No, it's something different,' Carrick left it at that.

Satisfied, Vullan nodded. 'Maybe you could tell Captain Shannon I'll visit him later. There are some details about tomorrow I want to check again. Dorothy –'

'Yes,' she agreed. 'We'd better move. What about John Marsh?'

Vullan shook his head. 'He's staying at the seaweed plant for the afternoon.'

They nodded good-bye. But as Vullan led Robert Chester away Dorothy Vullan hung back for a moment.

'Do you know anything more about last night, Webb?' she asked bluntly, her face serious.

'Nothing concrete,' he admitted. 'But –'

'I hope it stays that way,' she cut him short, her voice quiet and earnest. 'I mean that. I'm hoping Milne is right – once he has finished these trials it may all just fade away.'

'They've got the election to talk about for a day or two,' mused Carrick, not totally convinced. 'After that – I just don't know.' He smiled at her sympathetically. 'It could work out.'

'The Witch of the Isles is hard to forget.' She said it bitterly. 'That shotgun business was out of the past, even if it was only some drunk trying to frighten me. But it could go on from there – I know that too. I've seen the rowan branches on some of the boats, to fend me off. Then there are the others – the ones who have left baskets of fish on the jetty at the island in the night. You know why?'

He shook his head.

'The other old belief, it's those that give that get.' Her voice was tighter, strained. 'Some of the skippers have always asked for a witch's blessing on their boats. But that's tradition, it was never serious – till now. And I want it finished.'

Suddenly, the Witch of the Isles turned on her heel and

hurried to join the two men waiting at the door of the hall. She left with them without a backward glance.

Carrick stayed where he was for a long moment, disturbed by the vehemence that had been behind her words. Then, shrugging, he went out the same way. The elderly woman he'd seen earlier was carefully pinning a tablecloth so that it would hang down to ankle length at the front of the voters' roll table. When he smiled at her, she gave him a cautious nod. Everybody had their problems.

The *Sea Whip* had gone from the harbour by the time Carrick got back there. Thankfully, the second sound truck had also quit its location and he walked round past the dockers unloading the mailboat's cargo, heading for the repair slipway.

This time there was no grouping of spectators around the *Rachel*'s damaged hull and no work seemed to be in progress. But he saw Angus Grant and the bandaged figure of Willie MacLean standing under the shadow of the fishing boat's stern, and scrambled down to join them on the slime and weed-coated slipway. Their greeting was restrained, a deliberate nod from Angus Grant and a neutral sounding grunt from MacLean, whose face was partly hidden by the bandages.

'How do you feel now?' he asked MacLean.

'Singed at the edges,' answered MacLean with an acid humour. 'But it's better than being scraped off a bulkhead. I'm not complaining.' He scowled along the *Rachel*'s hull to the hole in her side. 'Not when I see what happened.'

'She'll mend,' said Angus Grant heavily. 'We'll maybe get one or two other wee jobs done too. I've told the lads, they'll be fishing again soon enough and in a better boat than before,'

'Don't say that too loudly when the insurance surveyor comes around,' said Carrick easily. He switched his attention to MacLean again. 'Where's the rest of your clan, Willie?'

'Up in the village, havin' a beer.' MacLean made a clumsy job of lighting a cigarette between his blistered lips. 'Skipper, if you're finished here I've got a thirst of my own.'

Grant nodded, but Carrick stopped the fishing hand as he turned to go.

'Tell Lachie I'd still like to know if he has any thoughts about who his friends were last night.'

'That?' MacLean shrugged slightly. 'I reckon we'll just take care of it on our own.'

He went off, and Carrick heard Angus Grant sigh. He watched the big, bearded fisherman run a hand down the *Rachel*'s hull, that weathered, beak-nosed face hard to read. Then, suddenly, Grant turned to face him.

'You had a busy time last night,' said Grant flatly. 'Here – and on the island. When Shona told me about that business with the shotgun –' Tight-lipped, he shook his head.

'It could get worse,' said Carrick bluntly. 'Someone might get really hurt next time.'

'No.' The word rasped from Grant. 'I – there are ways of making sure of that.'

'A few words in the right ears?' Carrick saw he wasn't going to get a response and nodded. 'Good. Does it also include ending the war with Dorothy Vullan?'

'Maybe that's another matter, Chief Officer,' said Grant curtly. 'A man's feelings are his own.' Then his manner changed. 'You'll have a dram with me tonight, when you come for Shona?'

'If it's offered,' said Carrick carefully.

'Aye.' An odd smile crossed the fisherman's face. 'It'll be waiting. That girl would give me hell if it wasn't.'

Carrick nodded good-bye, left him, and made his way back round the harbour to *Marlin*. An elderly M.G. coupé was parked beside the gangway. Though there was no clue to its owner, the petty officer on gangway watch stepped forward as he came aboard.

'Chief,' he began, 'Captain Shannon –'

'Wants me,' said Carrick resignedly.

He headed for the day cabin, knocked, waited for Shannon's grunt, then went in and gave a grin as he saw who their visitor was.

'Don't look so damned pleased,' said the man standing beside Shannon's rubber plant. 'I only came here for the car mileage.'

'And that maybe isn't a joke,' said Captain Shannon stonily. *Marlin*'s commander was also on his feet, but over by his desk, and the atmosphere in the room wasn't totally cordial.

They'd worked with Detective Inspector Malcolm Henderson before. He was thin and tall, had a dark, drooping moustache, and affected a habitually sad expression. As usual, he wore a leather jacket over slacks and a sweater but with a new acquisition, a long, hand-knitted wool scarf which reached down almost to his knees.

Carrick closed the cabin door and glanced at Shannon.

'I radioed Department and told them we could use some discreet assistance from the local police,' said Shannon, ignoring Henderson for the moment. 'Call it breaking a promise if you want, mister – to my mind that's incidental.'

'And my bosses sent me because I'm not known around Feanport,' contributed Henderson, unperturbed. 'The trouble is –'

'The trouble is, he wants everything laid on a plate,' snarled Shannon. 'Hard fact evidence all the way, or he isn't interested.'

'I didn't say that,' soothed Henderson. 'Suppose we re-run some of it now that Carrick is here?'

Shannon grunted and slumped down into a chair with an ill-tempered shrug. Flickering a grimace in Carrick's direction, Henderson cleared his throat.

'Start with Constable MacKenzie's death,' he began, all humour suddenly gone from his manner. 'There was the usual post mortem, with death certified due to drowning. Webb, the facts all fitted – MacKenzie took his boat out, it came ashore overturned. There's just one simple, natural conclusion, that he had an accident of some kind out there.'

'He was a good swimmer,' said Carrick quietly.

'Yes,' admitted Henderson.

'There's also where his body was washed up,' said Shannon curtly. 'He usually went fishing in the bay. He turns up on the rocks at Broch Point. How did he get down there?'

Henderson frowned uneasily. 'Captain, you admitted it could happen. That the tides and currents around here –'

'Made it possible, not probable,' snapped Shannon. 'There's a difference.'

Henderson shrugged. 'The medical examiners still said drowning, and up here they've plenty of experience in that area. The body was released to relatives and MacKenzie was cremated – finish. So next you've got his quarrel with Dorothy Vullan. She created hell at Headquarters about that break-in at the seaweed plant, but MacKenzie's story was that he hadn't any real proof who was responsible.'

'And afterwards?' queried Carrick.

'Nothing that Headquarters know about.' Henderson stuck his hands in the pockets of his leather jacket. 'Any prowling MacKenzie was doing, any questions he was asking about the Vullans or the *Sea Whip* was in his own time. I don't know what he was after and he didn't leave any hint behind him on paper. We've had his records brought in and checked as a matter of ordinary routine.'

'But what about the rest of it?' demanded Shannon wearily. 'The explosion on the *Rachel,* the shot fired at Fean House, every other damned thing that's going on around here? Do you want to just wait and see what happens next?'

'No. But I've got to hope the lid stays on things for another couple of days.' Henderson sucked at a stray end of his moustache and looked to Carrick for understanding. 'It's this lousy by-election – just about every spare cop we can scrape together is needed to stand sentry outside the official polling stations. They'll be there like so many wooden Indians and about as useful, but that's the law. Get the by-election out of the way and then we can move in. But not before, not unless all hell really breaks out.' He shrugged apologetically at Shannon. 'Sorry, but that's how it is.'

Shannon's answer was a low rumble of despair deep in his throat. Then he got to his feet.

'I saw a witchcraft panic once before, over the the north-east coast,' he said in a quiet, controlled voice. 'Years ago, when you and Carrick were probably still at school. An old, half-mad women cursed a boat and it sank in a gale, with all hands. I saw nets burned on the quayside, because crews thought they were bewitched. I saw grown men act like' – he paused and sucked his lips – 'well, they were ready to burn that woman like they'd burned the nets. Except a doctor had her certified and carted her off first.'

'And that's happening here could be different, maybe worse?' Henderson nodded slowly, with understanding. 'I'm not laughing, and I'll be back. Tomorrow if I can, but the day after that at the latest – and I'll maybe check a few things before then.'

Shannon studied him for a moment, his manner gradually thawing. Then he held out his hand.

'Do that,' said *Marlin*'s commander briefly. 'And tell your bosses they could have sent worse.'

'Thanks.' Henderson grinned, shook hands with him, and turned to Carrick. 'Walk with me to dry land?'

Carrick glanced at Shannon, drew a nod of agreement, and left the cabin with Henderson. The lanky detective inspector said nothing until they had reached the head of the gangway leading down to the quayside.

'Really got him, hasn't it?' he suggested dryly, stopping with his hand on the rail. 'How far do you go along with him?'

'All the way,' said Carrick.

'That just might make three of us.' Henderson scowled at the thought. 'Headquarters are going to love me when I log this one, Webb – but if there is anything behind it, your lady Witch of the Isles could be playing a funny game of her own. Don't lose sight of that one. Or that, from what your Old Man told me, the trouble seemed to start just around the time this character Marsh arrived on the scene.'

'You could check him out,' mused Carrick.

'You know, I'd never have thought of that,' said Henderson with a dry sarcasm. He took a deep breath of the harbour air and grinned. 'If I come up with anything, you owe me a drink.'

He headed down the gangway, climbed into his little car, and a moment later it snarled away along the quayside. As it vanished, Carrick turned and made his way up towards the bridge. His intention was to spend some time in the chartroom, seeing for himself what Shannon had said about the tides and current in the Brannan Sound. But as he reached the bridge he found Jumbo Wills and the fishery cruiser's radio operator huddled in consultation over a stripped-down piece of equipment.

'Mice?' queried Carrick mildly.

The radio operator grinned but Wills wasn't amused. His freckled face wore a worried look and one finger was gashed and bleeding where he'd cut it with a long, thin-bladed screwdriver.

'The echo-sounder's packed in,' he reported unhappily. 'I didn't notice till we were back in harbour, and I haven't even told the Old Man yet.' He chewed his lip anxiously. 'I was playing around with it when I had the watch and –'

'And now you'd better get it fixed before you tell him,' said Carrick. The echo-sounder did just that, threw a sound signal down from under *Marlin*'s keel, picked up the echo that bounced back from the sea-bed, and gave a depth reading vital in the kind of inshore patrol work which was the fishery cruiser's regular routine. 'What's gone wrong with the thing?'

Jumbo Wills sucked his bleeding finger and left the radio operator, a tow-headed youngster who spent his spare time playing Country and Western hit numbers on a home-made electronic guitar, to do the talking.

'Circuit overloads and a burn-out,' he said laconically. 'I can fix it – I think. If you want the technical detail, Chief –'

'No.' Hastily, Carrick shook his head then had second thoughts. 'Hold on. One question, one answer. Do you mean it got – well, some kind of electrical shock from outside?'

The youngster grinned and shook his head. 'No, nothing fancy like that.' He glanced at Wills. 'It's the kind of thing that happens if – uh – well, like the second mate says, he was playing around with it.'

'I see.' The answer was diplomatic but plain enough. Carrick had other problems. 'All right, but get it working.'

He left them, went to the chartroom, spent enough time there to understand Shannon's reluctant agreement that the tides and currents might take a body from the bay to Broch Point, then went back down to the main deck in time to see Clapper Bell walking back aboard. The burly bo'sun waved a greeting and came over.

'I had a wee bit o' luck, sir,' said Bell with a grin. 'I found that character Campbell, the rough-house expert, Shuggy Morrison told us about. He's workin' in a garage, like Shuggy said – we had a talk round the back, private.'

'It looks that way.' Carrick eyed the red bruise wealing one side of Bell's face. 'Friendly persuasion?'

'Self-defence,' said Bell with an outraged innocence. 'He hasn't my easy kind of nature.'

'His misfortune,' agreed Carrick sadly. 'Well?'

'He admitted he took a couple o' his pals along and jumped Lachie MacLean last night,' said Bell happily. 'But Campbell's story is they only intended to scare him an' that they ended up gettin' the biggest fright when we piled in. And – uh – he says it was Lampeye's idea.'

'Why?' asked Carrick, frowning.

'They reckon if they chase the MacLeans out o' Feanport they'll get their old jobs back on the *Rachel*.' Bell rubbed his chin, puzzled. 'Does that make any kind o' sense to you?'

'As much as anything has since we got here,' said Carrick. He used a thumbnail to pick at a blister of paint on the metal beside him. 'Apart from that, how do the MacLeans rate with the locals?'

'They don't mix much, keep out o' trouble – they just stay

outsiders.' Bell had something more important on his mind. 'You know, we did say we'd get some diving time while we were here. How about it – right now, this afternoon?'

Suddenly, it seemed a good idea. Carrick felt in need of some peace and underwater was as good a place as any to find it.

'Get the gear ready,' he nodded. 'I'll clear it with the Old Man.'

Captain Shannon agreed, in a way that made it plain he felt the same way too. Half an hour later, wearing black rubber wet-suits and with their scuba gear piled aboard, Carrick and Bell rasped their way out of the harbour aboard one of *Marlin*'s small outboard-powered Gemini boats.

As the little inflatable cleared the breakwater Clapper Bell swung her head north and opened the outboard's throttle. They foamed on, fairly close to the shore, and Clapper Bell pointed towards a small jetty and a huddle of buildings at the far end of the village. The work-boat with the strange bucket-grab at its bow was clue enough for Carrick and he took a long, curious look at the seaweed plant as they went past.

The north end of the bay came next, the narrow, shallow passage between the mainland and Fean Island. It was easy enough to imagine how it would dry out at low tide as they slowed and murmured through, the bottom rock and shingle clearly visible close beneath as the inflatable passed through and out beyond the white rim of surf which marked the start of the open sea.

The waves were bigger, the sea a deeper shade of blue as the outboard engine opened up again and drove them swiftly on along the empty, rugged coastline. Then, two miles north of the bay, their goal appeared ahead – a sea-cliff cove where the wreck-chart shielded on Carrick's lap marked the resting place of the *Martha Pym,* a torpedoed cargo ship and casualty of World War Two.

They brought the inflatable in, beached her at the foot of the cliff, then dragged the lightweight craft high and dry on the shingle. A white farmhouse on a distant hill and an off-shore stack of basalt rock gave them the compass marker points they needed.

It was to be a practice dive, nothing more. But Carrick and Bell still approached the drill involved with the total, careful routine which had long since become second nature. Once in their aqualung harness, the big twin air cylinders on their backs standard eighteen hundred p.s.i. jobs, they checked the air supply, fastened the weight belts round their waists, and were ready.

Carrick led the way, wading out, meeting the first, familiar chill of the sea as it seeped into the rubber wet-suit. The sea-bed sloped steeply, a few steps brought the slopping waves up to their chests, and Carrick paused, checking the compass on his wrist. Then, with a nod to Clapper Bell, he pulled on his face-mask, bit on the breathing tube, and duck-dived under.

They followed the sharp downhill slope of the sea-bed, demand valves clicking regularly, twin trails of air bubbles pluming from their masks while they finned along in a steady, kicking crawl-beat. The light faded slowly in the clear water, while small fish scattered from their path or darted into the shelter of the gently waving forest of long green kelp weed which beckoned from below.

Carrick's depth gauge registered ninety feet when the slope levelled out in a bottom layer of rock and weed. At that depth, it was a twilight world of undersea life, strange crawling shapes and flickering shadows. But suddenly, Clapper Bell kicked closer to him, tapped his shoulder, and pointed to their left.

They'd found the *Martha Pym*. In another minute they were swimming along the length of her broken hull.

The old cargo ship lay on her side, a single funnel which had broken loose lying half-buried in shingle and ooze, upper decks a shambles of broken, tangled fittings, the tip of one of her boilers protruding from a giant rent in her side. Swaying weed sprouted in profusion along her old-fashioned, riveted plates, which were encrusted with barnacles and limpet shell-fish.

Exploring on, they saw they weren't the wreck's first visitors. Her propeller had been cut away – commercial divers got good money for scrap bronze. And the *Martha Pym* had well-established tenants. As they reached the rent in her side a bad-tempered angler fish, a large, sharp-toothed mouth in a modest-sized body, came out to challenge their intrusion but disappeared again as Bell released an extra bout of air bubbles.

Any wreck along the north-west coast became home for a variety of creatures, from conger eel onward. A few young, innocent cod showed next, timidly following them as they continued to examine the rusting hull and reached the bridge, with its shattered glass and silt-covered controls.

At ninety feet, the standard diving tables gave a maximum underwater time of thirty minutes without decompression stops. Carrick let twenty minutes pass, then gestured to Bell and thumbed towards the surface. But Bell waved a negative, pointing down towards the sea-bed.

A large, fat lobster was scuttling along between the bottom weed. They finned down together then Bell grabbed the lobster in a sideways swoop and waved it triumphantly under Carrick's face-mask, like a trophy.

That was when it happened. Carrick had a glimpse of something that looked like a great, wide cloak sinking down on them from the twilight above, their escort of tiny cod tried to scatter, he saw Clapper Bell's eyes widen – and before either of them could attempt to kick clear a great swathe of weighted net enfolded them.

Settling mesh tangling around the air cylinders on his back, more of it catching at his arms and legs, Carrick was dragged down on his hands and knees among the bottom weed. The same thing had happened to Clapper Bell, who had tumbled just out of reach and was struggling to get up off his back.

For a moment, Carrick knew raw fear as the tough nylon wrapped itself more and more around him, end weights sending up clouds of sea-bed silt. Then, suddenly, he became conscious of his rasping, hurried breathing, felt a warning tightening in his throat, cursed himself for a fool, and stayed still for a moment.

Clapper Bell was doing the same. It was the grim discipline of underwater work. Never rush, think positively, breathe regularly. Carefully, tugging against the mesh, Carrick forced his right arm down until his fingers gripped the diving knife in his leg sheath.

Carefully, slowly, he used the sharp blade to saw through a first small section of mesh. That gave him more freedom and a better grip on the knife as he worked on, steadily gaining more slack, and gradually widening the hole in the mesh until his arm was free. Then, ignoring his numbed fingers, he began the steady process of hacking and sawing his way out of the net.

It took time, but he had company. Clapper Bell was busy

in the same way as the minutes dragged past. Carrick beat him to freedom, kicked across, and helped the burly bo'sun slash the last strands of mesh around his air-tanks. They were over their thirty minutes and Carrick tapped his watch for emphasis before he pointed upward.

They took their first decompression stop at twenty feet from the surface, where the water was bright and their arrival scattered a small school of silver mackerel. Then, resisting temptation, they shared another stop at ten feet – and finally they broke surface, spitting out their breathing tubes, shoving back their face masks.

The sea-cliff cove was empty. But out beyond it a small fishing boat was heading away, engine a murmur, hull little more than a black speck in the sea. Clapper Bell began cursing and Carrick's feelings were the same. It could be any boat. At that distance, there was no way they could ever identify it again.

They floated together for a moment longer, the speck still receding, then turned and swam back towards the shore.

The inflatable was where they'd left it and hadn't been touched. Rummaging in a haversack, Clapper Bell produced a flask of rum and they sat in silence on the shingle till it was finished.

'An' that turned out a real practice dive,' said Clapper Bell bleakly after another moment. 'What do you reckon? That they tracked our air bubbles then made their net cast?'

Carrick nodded, a cold shiver going up his spine at the memory. The weighted net had been a callous, deliberate attempt to trap them down there beside the *Martha Pym,* leave them to a horrifying, lingering wait for death.

Bell sighed, stuck a cigarette between his lips, and lit it with a grunt of sheer pleasure.

'Bastards,' he said conversationally. 'What do we do about it?'

'Remember,' said Carrick stonily. 'That's all we can do. Someone must reckon we're becoming a nuisance, asking too many questions.'

'You know the worst of it?' said Bell morosely. 'I lost my supper down there – that damned lobster.' He contemplated the peaceful water of the cove and his mouth twisted. 'I'll tell you this – I don't feel like goin' down for another one.'

CHAPTER SIX

It was dusk by the time Carrick and Bell motored the little Gemini inflatable back through the Feanport breakwater entrance and into harbour again. The mailboat had gone, a small, neat lighthouse supply tender flying the Northern Lighthouse Commissioners' flag had taken her place, and the last of the rapidly fading daylight was already being challenged by the street lamps in the village above.

Once they'd nudged alongside *Marlin*'s hull, Carrick left Clapper Bell to see to the Gemini being hoisted in. Going aboard, he started in search of Captain Shannon but met Jumbo Wills instead.

'He went ashore about half an hour ago,' Wills reported cheerfully. 'He wanted to talk to the skippers of those pair-trawl boats. Webb, they got that catch in and you should have seen it being landed! They had the buyers queuing.'

'That should make a happy time at the Anchor Watch tonight,' said Carrick, undismayed at the delay.

'I was thinking that,' said Wills wisely. His freckled face shaped a grin. 'Ferguson is duty officer tonight. How about you and I –'

'Another time,' said Carrick, shaking his head. 'Sorry. I've got plans.'

'I think I saw her in the village this afternoon,' said Wills sadly. Then he brightened again. 'Look, about that echo-sounder fault. It was some kind of overload and we had the spares to fix it. But – ah – I haven't mentioned it to the Old Man yet. So I was wondering –'

'I saw nothing, heard nothing, know nothing,' Carrick said flatly. 'But if you don't tell him, he'll find out.'

As Wills sighed and plodded off, Carrick headed aft towards his cabin. A few minutes later, having stripped off his black rubber scuba suit, showered, and dried himself down, he lay back on top of his bunk and relaxed for a spell, trying again to make sense out of what had happened out at the wreck of the *Martha Pym*.

It still came down to a frightening bid which could have

left them both to die under ninety feet of water. It had been no simple grudge against Fishery Protection – unless they were dealing with a madman. Which left only one other immediate possibility, that someone felt too many questions were being asked around Feanport.

Questions that were bringing very few sensible answers.

He gave up at last, rose, and dressed in shore-going civilian slacks, shirt and tie and a sports jacket. As he transferred money and other oddments to his pockets the cigarettes taped to the mirror tempted him again. On an impulse, he untaped one side of the packet, then quickly slapped the tape back in place and stood back as he heard a knock on the cabin door. The door swung open a moment later and Captain Shannon walked in.

'Shore rig, eh?' Shannon's eyes showed a brief, surprisingly humorous twinkle. Then, crossing over, he plumped down on the edge of Carrick's bunk. 'I've talked to Clapper Bell. Any notion why it happened?'

Carrick shook his head.

'Then don't waste your time asking around,' grunted Shannon. He drew out his cigarettes then scowled at the pack taped to the mirror and tucked his own away again. 'I forgot. You're still a non-smoking zone – a burden to the rest of humanity. Anyway, don't waste your time asking. I've just learned that lesson again.'

'The pair-trawl skippers?' queried Carrick.

Shannon nodded. 'Innocent faces and sly smiles. But your harbourmaster friend says they sent a box of fish across to Fean Island almost as soon as they berthed. A token of thanks to the Vullans.'

'And it's easy enough to guess why,' mused Carrick. 'Vullan more or less admitted it.'

'Yes.' Shannon sucked his lips then rubbed a hand over his beard. 'We know, mister. But as far as they were concerned who did they think they were really thanking? Milne Vullan or the Witch of the Isles?' He sighed. 'Enjoy your shore time, but try not to stir up anything. I'm going to stay in my cabin and pray no idiot gallops in to tell me he's seen something strange flying across the moon. God knows, we've had just about everything else.'

Carrick left *Marlin* at seven-thirty. It was a mild evening, the moon framed by thin wisps of cloud and the wind still light and from the west. Walking along the quayside, he passed a few groups of gossiping fishermen who were passing the time while their boats loaded ice and took on fuel and he noticed that the lighthouse supply tender at the north quay was preparing to sail.

The fishermen ignored him. But as he reached the harbour gates a car which had stopped outside flashed its headlamps at him. It was a dark blue Volvo station wagon and as he went towards it Milne Vullan and John Marsh climbed out. At the same time the driver's window was wound down and Dorothy Vullan smiled out at him.

'I thought it was you, Chief Officer,' she said triumphantly, then glanced scathingly at her husband and Marsh. 'Men – they didn't recognize you out of uniform.'

'My infallible wife,' murmured Vullan amiably and winked at Marsh, who grinned dutifully. 'Having the evening off, Carrick?'

'It could be my last chance here,' said Carrick, then paused. 'I didn't see your boat in the harbour.'

'We came across to the seaweed plant jetty,' explained Dorothy Vullan. 'I wanted to pick up the car. We keep it at the plant, and I'm having the evening off too, a gossip session with a girl who lives inland.'

'When Dorothy says "girl" she means any woman up to pensionable age,' said Vullan dryly.

'And any woman is a girl till she decides differently,' countered Dorothy Vullan crisply. She reached over and opened the passenger door. 'I'll give you a lift, Chief Officer. I think I know where you're heading.'

'It isn't far,' said Carrick mildly.

'Let her deliver you,' said Vullan and made a vague gesture. 'John and I have to visit that damned polling station again, to make sure everything's ready. It opens for business at eight a.m.'

'If anyone turns up,' mused Marsh, his lined face shaping a cynical doubt.

'Even Feanport has its political faithful,' frowned Vullan. 'They'll be there. But we might as well take care of things at the harbour, while we're here.'

'Like seeing a couple of fishing skippers?' queried Carrick.

Vullan chuckled. 'Maybe. But I promised Dorothy's friend Chester, the antique king, we'd double-check that his crates are properly stored. It'll be a couple of days before the truck arrives to move them south.'

'One man's junk, another man's fortune,' said Marsh caustically.

'So do I give you a lift or not?' said Dorothy Vullan with a slight impatience.

Obediently, Carrick boarded the Volvo. Starting the car, Dorothy Vullan set it moving and he had a last glimpse of her husband and Marsh heading in through the harbour gates. The Witch of the Isles drove with more zest than skill and Carrick winced as she took a corner with a squeal of tyre rubber.

'I saw Shona this morning and she said she was seeing you tonight,' explained Dorothy Vullan, unperturbed. She glanced sideways at Carrick, the car veering across the narrow road in the process. 'I'm fond of that girl. She's the only blood relative I've got.'

'Is that a warning?' asked Carrick mildly.

She laughed, gave a warning blast on the horn as a dog escaped from their path, then changed the conversation abruptly.

'Milne's made me a promise – no more fishing trials after this week. At least, not anywhere near Feanport, ever.'

'It should help,' mused Carrick, then winced as she took another corner. 'What about tonight?'

'I won't be late back, and John Marsh is staying at the house,' she said with an almost aggressive cheerfulness.

'Good.' Carrick was glad they were already almost at the end of the village. 'Your friend Chester get away on time?'

'He left hours ago,' said Dorothy Vullan. 'He planned to drive to Inverness to catch the evening plane out of there for London. It's a long drive, but he can make it and leave the hire car at the airport.' A slight edge entered her voice. 'Time is money to people like Robert Chester. I'll bet he already has customers lined up for every antique in those crates he brought back from the islands.'

As she spoke, she braked the Volvo and stopped it at the side of the road. Angus Grant's cottage was a short distance ahead, to the right of a fork in the road.

'I'm heading north,' she explained then grimaced. 'Anyway, it wouldn't help your popularity with a mule-head like Grant if he saw me dropping you off.' Then, suddenly, her hand rested lightly on Carrick's arm. 'You know, I reckon I was very lucky to find a man like Milne. Shona could use some happiness too – temporary or otherwise. That's all I'm going to say.'

She brushed aside Carrick's thanks, then set the blue station wagon moving again as soon as he got out. The Volvo took the left fork, swinging north, and as the red tail lights vanished Carrick walked the short distance down to the other road towards the cottage.

When he knocked on the door, Angus Grant opened it. The big, bearded fisherman was in his work clothes, which was a surprise, and had a new, almost aggressively brisk air as he invited Carrick in.

They went through to a small living-room furnished in a faded, old fashioned style but neat and clean and with a peat fire smouldering in a polished iron grate.

'You'll have a dram,' said Grant and made it a statement of fact, going over to a table where he had a bottle and glasses waiting. 'Shona says she's almost ready – though when a woman says that, it can mean anything.'

He poured the drinks neat, brought the glasses over, and smiled gravely as he saw Carrick looking at a framed photograph of an attractive, dark-haired woman in a wedding dress.

'Aye, that was my wife, Chief Officer. A bonnie woman – Shona had to get her looks from somewhere, eh?'

Carrick nodded, took the offered drink, raised the glass in a silent toast, and sipped the whisky. It had that clean, special edge which usually meant a high-grade illicit still.

'I'm leaving in a minute,' said Grant. 'Fishing again – I've arranged things with one of the local skippers. My own crew and his boat. She's the *Duchess,* a forty-footer, smaller than my *Rachel,* but better than none. He'll use her by day, I'll use her by night.'

'Shift work?' queried Carrick.

Grant grunted agreement. 'If it can be done with a factory, it can be done with a boat – for a spell, anyway, till the *Rachel* is ready. His crew need their rest, mine need the work.'

The room door opened as he finished and Shona came in. Carrick shaped his lips in a silent whistle of appreciation, liking what he saw. Long chestnut hair caught back in a silver clasp, she was wearing a figure-hugging cocktail dress of light cream wool, a tiny silver necklet on a thin chain at the throat. She was carrying a heavy Black Watch plaid shawl over one arm.

'Aye, you'll do,' said Angus Grant in a gruff, fatherly, compliment.

'Anywhere,' agreed Carrick.

She smiled at them, then faced Carrick.

'Ready when you are,' she said cheerfully.

Carrick finished his drink. Draping the shawl over her shoulders, Shona turned to her father.

'Be careful out there,' she said quietly. 'You'll be on a strange boat.'

'A boat is a boat and fish are fish, girl,' answered Grant patiently. 'We'll be back in before dawn.'

He went with them to the door then, as he said good night, Carrick stopped him.

'Any idea where the MacLeans were this afternoon?' Carrick made the question a casual one. 'I was looking for them.'

'I'm their skipper, not their keeper,' said Grant, some of the warmth fading from his voice. 'I couldn't tell you.'

He gave them a nod, went back into the cottage, and closed the door. Shona didn't seem to have noticed the change in mood. Taking Carrick's arm, she led the way round to the side of the house, where a small grey Volkswagen was parked.

'Borrowed – like father, like daughter,' she said, handing Carrick the keys. Her eyes twinkled in the moonlight. 'You drive, I'll navigate, and you'd better not count on eating for a spell. The only place I could think of is about twenty miles south of here.'

'I'll survive,' said Carrick with a grin, helping her in on the passenger side. 'I can always turn cannibal.'

She laughed and sat close to him once he'd got behind the wheel.

The road south was narrow, winding and varied between stretches that clung to spectacularly moonlit lengths of coastline and other sections that ran inland, between the hills and through passes blasted from the rock. Once the Volkswagen's headlamps showed a deer on the tarmac ahead for the brief instant before it raced off. Other wildlife abounded, from small scurrying rabbits to larger, anonymous shapes which were simply a momentary glimpse of a pair of bright eyes.

But the traffic was light, not much more than a few cars and an occasional giant refrigerated fish truck on the overnight haul to the cities. Carrick set a relaxed, unhurried pace and Shona was content to curl up on the seat beside him, saying little and equally at peace.

The twenty miles took about forty minutes, then a glow of lights showed ahead. Following his passenger's directions, Carrick turned off the road and the car crunched down a gravelled path. The path took a bend and ahead of them lay a long, low building, brightly lit, which faced out towards the silvered water of the Brannan Sound.

'That's it – the Clanstop,' said Shona, pointing ahead. 'One of the big hotel groups built it as a motel complex for the summer tourist trade. But the way things worked out, the bar and restaurant side keeps busy all the year round. Like I said, it's the only place you can eat out for miles around here.'

There was a well-filled car park to one side. Carrick coasted the Volkswagen towards it and found a parking slot, close to a sign that said 'Marina' and pointed down towards the shore. He smiled a little at that. There were a few places like the Clanstop being built along the coast, hoping to catch a share of everything from the winter ski-ing trade to the yachting extroverts who ventured that far north. But Shona was right. Most of them were surprised to find that their real business came from the locals – who had year-round money and a new generation outlook about what to do with it.

They locked the Volkswagen and left it, heading towards the Clanstop's neon-topped doorway. But halfway across, Carrick slowed and gave an involuntary grunt of surprise.

'Something wrong?' asked Shona, puzzled.

'Stone in my shoe,' Stooping, he made a show of flicking a piece of gravel out of one shoe then rose, took her arm, and they went on.

But he'd taken the chance to have a second glance and he'd been right. Dorothy Vullan's dark blue Volvo station wagon, the car she'd taken out of Feanport saying she was heading north to visit a friend, was parked in the row next to the one they were passing.

Which, Carrick told himself, might be none of his business. Except that after the last couple of days he was left with a feeling that he couldn't afford to ignore anything that concerned the Witch of the Isles.

In another moment they were in the carpeted warmth of the Clanstop's lobby. There were clan badges on the walls and the drapes were tartan but everything else was chrome and plastic. The motel section was to the left, the main bar, softly lit and with music coming from it, was to the right, and the restaurant doorway was straight ahead.

Still thinking about what he'd seen, Carrick steered Shona towards the bar, where a waitress in a tartan mini-kilt and a cutaway blouse found them a table. The place was as busy as the car park had suggested, crammed by a mixture of young farmers and fishermen and their girls plus a sprinkling of army men in from a mountain warfare course. The blast of music came from a guitar, bass and drums trio with an electronic hook-up and the postage-stamp sized dance floor was filled.

'It isn't exactly candlelight and quiet,' said Shona almost apologetically, 'but –'

'I like it,' he said easily. 'Show me some food soon and I could even get to love it.'

He ordered drinks, and by the time the waitress brought them he had made sure that Dorothy Vullan wasn't anywhere in the crush. But she was still very much on his mind. Paying for the drinks, he shoved back his chair.

'Two minutes and I'll be back,' he promised. 'If I go missing, try the men's room.'

She laughed and nodded and Carrick went back out into the lobby. Going across to the restaurant entrance, he reserved a table and looked around the diners at the same time. Again, there was no sign of Dorothy Vullan.

That left the motel section and he turned towards it then hesitated, telling himself again it could be none of his business.

Next moment, cursing under his breath, he took a quick side-stepping shuffle behind the shelter of a display stand boosting the tourist attractions available around the Clanstop's location. Dorothy Vullan had just emerged from the corridor which led to the motel rooms – and the man by her side was Robert Chester, who should have been on that night plane out of Inverness on his way to London and his antique deals.

The couple went straight across the Clanstop lobby and out into the night, towards the car park. Carrick stayed where he was, making a pretence of studying the display board, and after a couple of minutes Chester returned alone and vanished back down the same corridor.

Feeling like a tame spy, Carrick in turn went out into the

night and walked over to where the Volvo had been parked. The space was empty.

He forced a grin back on his face when he returned to the bar and joined Shona again. When they'd finished their drinks they went through to the restaurant where the food and service was good but the menu prices were high to match. He joked and talked his way through the meal, but what he'd seen was still on his mind and it must have shown. He caught Shona eyeing him oddly a few times, but she made no direct comment.

Afterwards, they went back into the bar, staying there for another drink and a few dances, and in the process he got Dorothy Vullan out of his thoughts. It wasn't too hard, he decided, as the calm grey eyes opposite met his own.

It was around midnight when they left. Carrick was driving the Volkswagen north again along the same empty road when whatever patience Shona Grant possessed suddenly snapped.

'Webb, I want to know what happened back there,' she said unexpectedly. 'Something did – I know that much, and I want to hear about it.'

Carrick gave a sideways glance. Her face, softly lit by the instrument lights, showed a firm determination. He shrugged, then sought a handy refuge from the truth.

'Sorry. I started thinking – about that character with the shotgun last night and what's maybe going to happen next.' He paused, taking the car round a sharp bend, then added grimly, meaning it, '*Marlin* sails from Feanport after tomorrow. That could be like taking the lid off the pot and I don't like the idea of your still being around.'

She moistened her lips. 'That's all?'

'I'd call it enough,' he said wryly.

She sat still for a moment, saying nothing, her face grave, watching the grey ribbon of road in the headlamps.

'Webb, pull in,' she said suddenly.

He stopped the car on the verge and waited. She looked at him carefully, as if reaching a decision.

'Take me home,' she said at last and gave him a quiet smile. 'If we've only tonight, I don't want to waste it.'

He leaned over, kissed her, then started the car again.

It was almost one a.m. by the dashboard clock when the lights of Feanport showed ahead and minutes later Carrick let the Volkswagen coast to a stop outside the darkened little cottage. Shona got out of the car first, waited until he joined her, then took his hand.

They were a few paces away from the front porch of the cottage when a figure stepped out of its shadow.

'Hello, Webb,' said a dry, all too familiar voice. It was Ferguson, and he was in uniform. The middle-aged junior second mate had a veiled grin on his dried-up face as he came forward. He nodded politely to Shona then turned to Carrick. 'I don't expect you to like this, but I've been hanging around that porch since midnight. The Old Man wants you back aboard.'

'Now?' Carrick glared at him.

'Right now. The moment you show up.' Ferguson glanced sideways at Shona. 'Sorry if it breaks up your evening, but –' He gave a thin-shouldered shrug and ended it there.

Carrick mentally damned Ferguson and Shannon with an equal ferocity. But there was nothing he could do about it.

'Tell him I'm on my way,' he said bleakly.

Ferguson gave a nod, and strode off briskly. Sighing, Carrick turned and looked at Shona in the moonlight.

'You'd better go,' she said, then gave a wry smile. 'But tell your captain he just lost a lot of popularity.'

He managed a resigned grin, kissed her lightly, then hurried down the street after Ferguson.

Marlin seemed as dark and silent at her quayside berth as the other vessels around the harbour. But a petty officer was waiting just beyond the gangway as the two officers came abroard and directed them straight away to the fishery crusier's tiny wardroom.

The deadlights had been closed over its portholes, it was brightly lit, and Captain Shannon was seated at the head of the wardroom table with some scribbled notes in front of him. There was a coffee pot on the table and some used cups around it showed that the wardroom had seen an earlier meeting.

'About time,' said Shannon scathingly as they entered. His eyes showed a lack of sleep but the small bearded figure was otherwise aggressively alert. 'Sit down, both of you.'

Obediently, Carrick and Ferguson took two of the chairs, settled, and waited. Ferguson still had the same expression of quiet amusement on his face, but whatever he knew, he said nothing.

'We've had a visitor,' said Shannon flatly. He lit a cigarette with a match and tossed the match into an already overflowing ashtray. 'Morrison the harbourmaster came sneaking aboard late tonight.' He paused, his expression hard to read. 'Morrison claims you threatened him, mister.'

'Unfortunately, he doesn't have any witnesses – apart from our bo'sun,' murmured Ferguson, his grin taking a cynical twist.

'And I don't give a damn,' grunted Shannon. 'Morrison says there's a fishing boat leaving harbour at five a.m. to help Vullan on a fishing trial.'

Carrick stiffened. 'Does he knew where?'

'No,' admitted Shannon. 'But she's the *Sandworm,* one he has used before – and the skipper has already loaded a trammel net supplied by Vullan. The net must be laid by six a.m. and the *Sandworm* is to head back to harbour.' He took a slow, frowning draw on his cigarette. 'I presume that means Vullan will show up just after that. Tomorrow is one day when he can't waste time.'

Carrick nodded agreement. With the Feanport polling station opening at eight a.m., Milne Vullan had a tight schedule ahead. But the trammel net, a long, floating curtain of mesh which could be paid out and left buoyed, was one type of fishing gear that could be collected later.

'I'd like to be out there,' he said softly.

'You're going to be,' said Shannon bluntly. 'I want that net checked, I want to know what happens when Vullan comes along – and I don't want him to know he has an audience. You'll have the patrol launch, with Ferguson and a couple of hands as surface back-up.'

Ferguson nodded. 'Clapper Bell is briefed, the scuba gear is already in the launch. I've picked two men and –'

'And the rest can wait,' Shannon cut him short and looked up at the wardroom clock. 'We'll make it an 0430 muster. That, Mister Carrick gives you about three hours' sleep.' He paused, and for a moment his bearded face showed a trace of amusement. 'That's maybe not what you had in mind when Ferguson found you, but that's the way it's going to be.'

Three hours in his bunk was better than none. But Carrick didn't find it easy to sleep. He lay in his cabin, part of his mind puzzling again and again over Dorothy Vullan's meeting with Robert Chester, the rest of his thoughts on

Shona Grant. He could still picture the moment Ferguson had stepped out of the shadows at the cottage porch, a moment when he could cheerfully have strangled him.

But sleep did come. And it seemed only minutes later when a seaman shook him awake again. Yawning, Carrick gulped down the mug of coffee the man left him, then pulled on a sweater and slacks and went on deck.

The fishery cruiser still lay dark and silent under the faint moonlight. The temperature seemed to have dropped too and he shivered slightly, listening to the creak of their mooring lines and the soft lap of the sea against the hull. Then he spotted a small group of figures huddled below the bridge and joined them. The first he recognized was Clapper Bell, who winked a greeting but said nothing, then Ferguson pushed his way forward

'It's starting,' said Ferguson in a low voice. 'The *Sandworm* is over on the north quay, to your left. The crew seem to be arriving.'

Carrick looked across the harbour and saw tiny, moving lights twinkling aboard one of the black shapes of the fishing fleet.

'Anything else?' he asked quietly.

'One boat came in about half an hour ago and tied up.'

He nodded. 'The *Duchess* – Grant had her out. What about her crew?'

'They went ashore,' shrugged Ferguson, then gave a satisfied grunt as the first sound of an engine starting up came from the other quay. 'Not long now. I'll let the Old Man know.'

He went away and returned in a couple of minutes with Captain Shannon, who was still in his pyjamas with a duffel coat over his shoulders and the pyjama legs stuffed into seaboots.

Another few minutes passed. Then the *Sandworm*'s navigation lights came on, her engine note changed, and she began easing away from her berth. They watched in silence as the fishing boat headed out of the harbour but as her stern lights passed the breakwater Shannon came to life.

'Now,' he rasped. 'And keep it quiet.'

The group of seamen around sprang into action and the patrol launch was quickly and carefully lowered. She was hardly in the water before Ferguson and his two deck hands were aboard, followed by Carrick and Clapper Bell. Ferguson started the engine with little more than a whisper of sound, they cast off, and in another moment they were inching away from *Marlin* with Shannon still watching from above.

A black shadow in the night, running without lights, the patrol launch murmured out past the breakwater. To the south, the *Sandworm* was a silhouette in the moonlight as she headed down the coast, gathering speed, and in the little cockpit of the patrol launch Ferguson glanced at Carrick and raised a questioning eyebrow.

'It's follow my leader,' Carrick told him. 'Keep your distance – just don't lose visual contact.'

One of the crewmen was at the helm, the other was already checking their radio link with *Marlin.* Both were among the fishery cruiser's most experienced hands, and the patrol launch, with her low, compact lines, had been designed for just his kind of work. Carrick had little fear of the *Sandworm* spotting the fact that she was being shadowed. He glanced around the cockpit again, past the echo-sounding gear to the compact, short-range radar. Neither was much use on this mission. Visual contact was more important – when the fishing boat got to work it was going to matter to know exactly what she did.

He left Ferguson and went below, into the tiny cabin, where Clapper Bell had begun the task of getting into his scuba suit. Carrick did the same, working by the dim light of a shaded bulb, while the patrol launch murmured on, pitching a little as it cleared the bay and met the more boisterous swell of the Brannan Sound.

When they had finished, they relaxed. Occasionally, Ferguson stuck his head down into the cabin to report progress. The fishing boat ahead kept to a southerly course, keeping to the middle of the Sound, and the only real change was that after twenty minutes her running lights blinked out.

Clapper Bell dozed. Carrick, too, felt his eyes gradually begin to close as the murmuring rhythm of the launch engine continued unchanged. Then, suddenly, it altered, slowed, and Ferguson stuck his head down again.

'We've arrived,' said Ferguson briefly. 'Better come up.'

He kicked Clapper Bell awake and they went up into the cockpit. The patrol launch was almost drifting in the swell and the *Sandworm* was clearly visible about half a mile ahead, moving slowly and making a curving turn to starboard.

'Position?' asked Carrick.

Ferguson gave a humourless grin. 'She's just east of the Witchrock – we should have guessed it.'

One of the crewmen gave a grunt, and handed Carrick glasses he'd been using. Carrick brought them up and trained them on the fishing boat, seeing the tiny figures working near her stern then the white streaking of disturbed water which told the rest. The trammel net was being laid.

They stayed clear, watching, until the fishing boat was finished. Then, at last, the *Sandworm* began heading for home and went past them, the beat of her engine loud across the water.

'Six a.m.' said Ferguson dryly, glancing at his watch. 'Like a railway timetable – only better. Our turn?'

Carrick nodded. The patrol launch began moving again and soon they were close to the bobbing line of marker floats which supported the waiting trammel net. Quickly, Carrick and Bell got into their scuba harnesses, made a last check of their gear, and clipped on the underwater lamps which had been added for the occasion. Then, when they were ready, Carrick beckoned Ferguson nearer.

'Remember Vullan is on his way,' he said grimly. 'If the *Sea Whip* shows while we're down –'

'I'll ease off and collect you later,' nodded Ferguson. 'I'll be on radar watch.'

Pulling down his facemask, Carrick signalled to Clapper Bell and they went into the water, duck-diving down to about twenty feet then switching on the underwater lamps to get their bearings. The fine, wavering curtain of the trammel net showed immediately and Carrick ventured right up to it.

As far as he could see, it was an ordinary net with an ordinary mesh. A solitary dogfish had already been trapped in it near where Clapper Bell was making a similar examination, the fish wriggling in the pool of light from Bell's lamp.

But Vullan had supplied the net. Carrick kicked his way over to join Bell, signalled, and they dived deeper, down to the heavy bottom rope. Then they stopped, equally puzzled. A small cylinder of white plastic, about half the size of a beer can, was attached to the rope by a plastic toggle. Bell finned to the left, exploring, then came back and beckoned, leading him further along the net. Another of the white plastic cylinders was there, but mounted higher up.

They parted, Carrick swimming to the left, Bell taking the righ-hand sector. It was a slow process, but by the time Carrick reached his end of the trammel net he had located six more of the plastic cylinders. Treating the close proximity of the mesh with much respect, he cut one of the cylinders loose with his diving knife, shoved it into the pocket of his scuba suit, and moved clear before he began swimming back towards the centre.

As he swam, he suddenly found himself shivering, ignored it, then realized something else was happening, an odd, singing sensation had begun building in his ears. The shivering increased and, puzzled, he checked his air supply, found it normal, and had begun to swim again when a silver shape like a small torpedo slammed into his body.

It was a large cod, and it blundered off him, swimming straight into the net. Almost immediately, other fish were around him, all heading in the same direction, some colliding with him, while the shivering sensation began to rack his body and the singing in his ears became a high-pitched wail.

And the fish came on, large and small, fleeing from an unknown something in a way that sent them into the waiting net as if it didn't exist. For Carrick, they were just one more element in a nightmare which still held no pain, only shaking bewilderment and a total weakness while he felt his body go out of control.

Bemused, he stared at the way the plume of air bubbles from his scuba mask had begun to bend and curve. It was a moment before his disorientated mind fought through to what that meant, that he was rolling over and over in the water. When he tried to right himself, the air bubbles began to dance while he slipped sideways instead, like a drunken doll.

Then suddenly, it was over. The shivering died, the singing vanished from his ears, all that was left was a total exhaustion and a sickness. Ignoring the curtain of trapped, struggling fish, mustering what strength he had left, he struck upwards, towards the surface.

As soon as his head was above water he tore off his face mask and vomited. It was a moment or two before he even remembered Clapper Bell – and then a retching noise from his right and the sight of another head bobbing on the surface not far away showed that Bell had been affected in exactly the same way.

Yet otherwise the sea was empty apart from the bobbing, mocking floats of the net.

Too exhausted to talk, they swam towards each other, cracked the little CO^2 cylinders which inflated their life vests, then lay back and floated, waiting.

It was ten minutes before the patrol launch nosed in and picked them up. They had to be practically dragged aboard then, while the two crewmen helped them out of their scuba gear, Carrick managed a weak grin as Ferguson bent over him.

'What the hell happened to you?' demanded Ferguson, his thin face tight with anxiety.

'It can keep,' Carrick told him in a dull voice. 'What about up here?'

'Vullan,' said Ferguson. 'Almost as soon as you went under we picked up a radar trace on the five mile scan, heading here fast. I eased clear, like we arranged then – well that damned *Sea Whip* stopped about half a mile off, then manoeuvred back and forward as if she was trailing something.' He shrugged. 'Four or five minutes of that, then he just got under way again, slamming back to Fean-port.'

'Four or five minutes?' Carrick echoed the words in near disbelief. Under the water, it had seemed an age. 'Anything else, anything at all?'

'Well, – Ferguson hesitated and scowled – 'just one thing I can't understand. We were using the echo-sounder, because we were on the edge of the channel and –'

'And it packed in? Total failure?' Carrick struggled up on his elbows, staring at him.

Ferguson nodded.

'We've been conned,' said Carrick bitterly. 'Shannon, all of us – we've been conned.' He dragged the white cylinder out of his thigh pocket and stared at it. 'Electic fish-herding – like hell it was.'

'What do you mean?' asked Ferguson, bewildered.

'I mean we get back to *Marlin* and dig the Old Man out of his bunk,' grated Carrick.

Clapper Bell was fumbling with a pack of cigarettes.

'I'll have one,' said Carrick.

'You've stopped,' croaked Bell.

'Mind your own damned business,' Carrick told him,

then grabbed a cigarette and lit it. 'This is medicinal.'

Ferguson gave up, turned, and nodded to the crewman at the controls. Shuddering to life, the patrol launch swung round and began carving a broad white wake as it headed back towards Feanport.

Dawn comes late in the northern Scottish winter. There was still just the beginning of an iron-grey hint of light on the horizon when the patrol launch slipped into harbour, came quietly alongside *Marlin,* and was smoothly hoisted in.

Ferguson had radioed ahead. As soon as Carrick and Bell were aboard they were summoned to Captain Shannon's day cabin where that small, fiery individual stared at them for a moment under the light. Then he swore softly and angrily.

'Sit down before you fall down, both of you,' he ordered with a frown that came close to concern. 'That damned fool Ferguson only said you'd had problems, not that you looked half-dead.' As they obeyed, he brought out glasses and a fresh bottle of his prized single-malt, then poured two of the largest whiskies either of them had ever seen. Then came another order. 'Get those into you.'

They did, while Shannon watched in silence. Then he nodded.

'All right, report.'

'Vullan isn't electric fishing. He's using high-frequency sound, ultrasonics – something like that,' said Carrick wearily. He handed a disbelieving Shannon the white cylinder he'd cut from the trammel net. 'Whatever is inside that thing should prove it.'

Shannon hefted the cylinder, chewed his lip, then shrugged. 'Well, if we're thieving, let's see what we've got.'

It took a knife to cut the plastic seal but after that the cylinder unscrewed and out fell a small, metal-cased box which might have been a photographic light-meter – except that it wasn't and the needle on the tiny dial had stopped at a scale reading.

'You said sound.' Shannon's voice grated on the word. 'Go on, mister.'

Carrick did, while Clapper Bell nodded an occasional agreement and Shannon's attitude gradually shifted from initial scepticism and silence to thawing acceptance and an occasional question. When Carrick finished, Shannon paced the cabin for a moment then suddenly swore, headed for the bookshelf beside his desk, and pulled out a thin, black-bound book. Apparently ignoring them, he thumbed the pages while Clapper Bell sat with his eyes almost closed and Carrick fought down an urge to yawn and keep yawning. Whatever had happened to them, Carrick had never felt so tired and weakened in his life.

Shannon turned, saw them, and said searchingly, 'Can you two stay awake long enough to listen for a moment?'

They straightened a little and nodded. Grunting, Shannon slapped the book shut.

'Extracts from papers at a recent oceanology conference in Boston,' he said. 'One of them is on sound, fish behaviour and fishing. Experiments on the use of specially designed fishing gear with a low underwater noise level – so that it doesn't frighten the fish away.'

Clapper Bell gave a semblance of a grin. Shannon saw it and sniffed.

'Bo'sun, I'm about to improve your education. Fish can hear – you know that much. It happens they can hear damned well. On a calm day they'll hear a ship's propeller when the ship is miles away. Some of the marine boffins have proved that a fish can even hear an aircraft flying over its patch of water – and I don't mean just low-level stuff.' He glanced at Carrick. 'Agreed, mister?'

Carrick nodded slowly. He didn't know much about it, but it was certainly long established that fish 'talked' underwater. He'd once heard a tape recording of twitters and grunts which amounted to the courtship build-up for one species. Other fish were said to home in on sounds when searching for prey.

'Mind you, as usual, the fishermen knew it long before the boffins made a fuss,' grunted Shannon. 'When I was a boy, any fisherman bringing a net alongside got a lad to thump on the side of the boat with a hammer – so that the noise would scare the fish, keep them in the net till it closed. But this –' He shook his head. 'How far from the net was the *Sea Whip* when it happened?'

'Ferguson says about half a mile,' said Carrick.

'My God,' says Shannon softly. 'And Vullan talked about small-scale field trials. If it still knocked hell out of you two –'

'An' blew the echo-sounder, sir,' reminded Clapper Bell sleepily.

'I hadn't forgotten.' Shannon gave a scowl. 'I'm going to have a talk with our Mr Wills about the first time that happened – which he still hasn't bothered to mention.' He drew a deep breath. 'Stay quiet about this for now, both of you. We've satisfied our own curiosity about what Milne Vullan is doing. No wonder those damned fishing skippers didn't believe his prattle about electric fishing – not when this sort of thing was happening.'

'But it doesn't change anything else,' said Carrick quietly.

'No, it doesn't,' agreed Shannon and shook his head. 'They'd call it witchcraft, mister. There's a whole village ripe for trouble around this harbour. What's happened already could be nothing compared with –' He stopped short and shook his head again. 'That's enough for now. Get out of here. Just looking at you is making me feel tired.' He paused and added almost absently, 'You did a fairly good job, both of you.'

Which Carrick decided, ranked close to a citation. They left the day cabin, parted, and he yawned and stumbled his way aft.

When he reached his own cabin, he had to fumble to open the door. He managed to close it again, reach the bunk, and then his legs buckled.

Still fully dressed, he was probably asleep before his head landed on the pillow.

CHAPTER SEVEN

Jumbo Wills wakened Carrick at noon and didn't find it easy. At last, cursing between yawns, Carrick levered himself out of the bunk, crossed to the cabin mirror, and scowled at the unshaven, bleary-eyed face that stared back at him.

'Do you feel as bad as you look?' asked Wills politely.

'Go to hell,' Carrick told him sourly.

'The company couldn't be worse there than it is around here,' retorted Wills indignantly. 'Maybe you had a rough time, but I've been skinned and gutted by the Old Man –'

'The echo-sounder business?' Carrick grinned.

'That, and anything else he could think up,' complained Wills. 'Now we've got Detective Inspector Henderson back aboard. He's with the Old Man, and they want to see you.'

Carrick raised an eyebrow. 'Why?'

Wills shrugged. 'I forgot. You wouldn't know. That little character Lampeye was fished out of the harbour this morning, drowned. Looks like he got stoned last night and –'

'You're sure it was Lampeye?' demanded Carrick, cutting him short, the news jarring him totally awake.

'I was there when they carted him off,' nodded Wills, and grimaced. 'He'd been jammed between the quayside and one of the fishing boats.'

'Tell the Old Man I'll be along directly,' said Carrick grimly.

Wills nodded and went out, banging the cabin door behind him. Going over to the cabin porthole, Carrick looked out. The sky was almost clear of cloud, the harbour scene appeared unchanged – almost peaceful. But now, after the reality of his own personal nightmare, Lampeye was dead.

He washed and shaved quickly, stripped off the crumpled clothes he'd slept in, and got back into uniform. Then, taking a deep breath, he set off to answer Shannon's summons.

Captain Shannon and Malcolm Henderson were standing at a table, studying a chart, when Carrick reached them. They broke off as he entered the day cabin, Shannon scrutinizing him carefully, the tall, thin policeman contenting himself with a twist of a smile from under his dark, drooping moustache.

'Fit for duty?' asked Shannon after a moment. 'The truth, mister.'

Carrick nodded and a glance that held a shade of relief passed between the other two men.

'You've heard about Lampeye?' queried Henderson.

'Yes.' Carrick glanced at the chart. It was the one Captain Shannon had used to map out his ballet box collection run. 'So – what happened?'

Henderson shrugged. 'He turned up when one of the fishing boats started to move out not long after first light. We know he was drinking heavily last night, we know he usually ended up sleeping it off somewhere around the harbour – that's about it so far.'

'Except this time I imagine the post mortem will be toothcomb style,' said Shannon with a sarcastic edge.

'It will.' Henderson's thin face flushed a little. 'We don't make the same mistake twice.'

'Twice?' Carrick seized on the word.

'George MacKenzie,' admitted Henderson. 'I've talked to the pathologist who performed the autopsy. He – well, he admits a couple of small details puzzled him.'

'How small?'

'Signs of a fairly hefty blow to the head, and some small cuts on the soles of his feet, as if he'd been walking barefoot on rock.' Henderson sucked an end of his moustache defensively and scowled. 'But he could have taken a crack on the skull when he went overboard, anything can happen to a body when it's in the water – and there's no doubt about the thing that matters, Webb. He drowned.'

'But how?' grunted Shannon.

Henderson flared at the inference. 'Captain, that's on my mind too. It also happens he was a cop, so don't get any notion that it doesn't matter to me.'

'We know it does,' soothed Carrick while the two men glared at each other. 'Look, come back to Lampeye. There's at least one major difference. MacKenzie was feuding with Dorothy Vullan, but Lampeye was working for her husband. There's no chance of the Witch being blamed this time by the gossip squads.'

'I wouldn't bank on it.' Henderson had a sad doubt in his voice. 'Take a walk past the harbour gates, Webb. There's a new slogan painted on a wall up there – "Burn the Witch".'

'That could have been any small boy with a paintbrush,' muttered Shannon. He rested his knuckles on the table, frowning absently. 'All right, we won't know till the post mortem. But the odds are that Lampeye's death was the way it looks, an accident. I still feel slightly better knowing what Vullan has really been doing out there – and that it's probably just about over now.'

'This ultrasonic fishing stuff?' Henderson rammed his hands in the pockets of his leather jacket and scowled. 'Maybe it explains a few things, but that's all.'

A fishing boat glided past the day cabin's window, heading out to sea, and the three men watched in silence until she had passed. Then Carrick had a question of his own.

'Did you check out John Marsh and the MacLean tribe?' he asked Henderson.

'I did, and so far I haven't got anywhere,' shrugged Henderson. 'I'm still trying.'

'Do me a favour,' said Carrick slowly. 'Add Robert Chester, a London antique dealer, to the list.' He saw Shannon raise an eyebrow and added cautiously, 'Dorothy Vullan met him last night – that's maybe none of our business, but I'm curious about him.'

'Will do,' sighed Henderson. 'As for the rest of it, I'm still hoping that today's damned election will keep most people quiet for a spell.'

'It helps,' grunted Shannon. 'At least we know where Milne Vullan will be most of the day. As local Returning Officer he'll have to stay close to the Feanport polling station.'

'Where I've got two large Highland constables on official duty,' said Henderson with a faint grin. 'Vullan's there right now, with his wife – I looked in on the way here.'

'And the polling stations stay open until nine tonight.' Shannon eyed Carrick thoughtfully, and tugged at his beard for a moment. 'Mister, we'll be sailing an hour before that time, on the islands vote collection run. We won't be back much before midnight.'

Henderson nodded. 'I'm going to try to be around, Webb. But I told you before, until tomorrow there's not as much as a spare police cadet available.'

Carrick said nothing, waiting, but with a feeling he knew

what was coming. A moment later, Shannon confirmed it.

'You look like you could use a little extra time ashore, mister,' said Shannon dryly. 'I'm going to leave you behind. You'll have the bo'sun and a couple of hands – call it a shore patrol, if you like. But you'll also have the patrol launch, and we'll think up a cover story so the whole thing doesn't look too obvious.'

'Settled,' said Henderson gladly. He glanced at his wristwatch and grimaced. 'I've got work to do, but I'll try to get back to Feanport before dusk, and I should have the post mortem report on Lampeye by then.' He grinned at Shannon. 'Thanks again.'

He left the cabin. Once the door had closed, Shannon settled in a chair and gave a sigh which held some relief.

'The *Sandworm* went out again at daylight and brought back Vullan's trammel net,' he said soberly. 'They landed the fish, then returned the net to Fean Island. I did something too, mister. I radioed a report to Department – in code, telling them what happened.' His mouth tightened. 'I've had a reply, though I didn't tell Henderson. I've been more or less told to mind my own damn business.'

Carrick frowned. 'So maybe they knew about it already?'

'Perhaps.' Shannon built a slow, deliberate steeple with his stubby fingertips and considered it. 'High frequency sound, ultrasonics – maybe you were luckier than you knew this morning. If that's what Vullan is working with, it's a damned dangerous tool.'

'They use it in medicine – and industry,' mused Carrick.

'And you can cut a man's throat with a scalpel,' snapped Shannon. 'You don't fool around with ultrasonics.' He paused, and his manner changed. 'I'll get Clapper Bell to spread the word we're leaving some people ashore to make sure there's no hitch when we bring those ballot boxes back – it's weak, but it'll do. I'll think up an excuse for the patrol launch later. Eaten yet?'

'No, sir.'

'Do that,' said Shannon. 'Then you're off watch as far as this ship is concerned.' A faint twinkle showed in his eyes. 'If you happen to meet a certain young woman, that's none of my damned business – as long as you remember the rest of what you're supposed to do.'

It was three o'clock by the harbour clock when Carrick went ashore. A lobster boat was unloading its catch but otherwise it was a quiet spell on the quayside, a few fishermen mending nets or washing down decks while transistor radios blared tinny music from a couple of fo'c'sles. Shuggy Morrison was standing at the door of the harbourmaster's office. He gave Carrick a dour nod, turned on his heel and went in. Grinning, Carrick walked on, passed the harbour gates, then stopped short.

'Burn the Witch.' The painted slogan Malcolm Henderson had talked about was daubed in almost man-sized letters on a wall just ahead. As he stared at it, he heard a chuckle and turned.

'It's a notion, isn't it, Chief Officer?' Hands in his pockets, a sardonic grin on his face, Donnie MacLean strolled towards him from a group of fishermen. The lanky fishing hand swept back a lock of his long dark hair then thumbed at the writing. 'Daft – but it might get as many votes as anything those politicians are brayin' about.'

'It's one way of wasting good paint,' Carrick eyed him stonily. 'Where's the rest of your clan?'

'Brother Willie had to go to the hospital to get those burn dressings changed – cousin Lachie went with him,' shrugged MacLean. 'Still, what's a burn or two? You heard about old Lampeye?'

Carrick nodded.

'It's gettin' so it's even unlucky to work for the Witch,' said MacLean and jerked his head towards the other fishermen, who had slowed, waiting on him. 'At least, that's what the lads are sayin'.'

'Tell them not to say it too loudly, or they might have problems,' Carrick told him pointedly. 'How did Angus Grant make out with his borrowed boat last night?'

MacLean grimaced. 'We didn't bring back enough fish to pay the fuel bill. But we'll keep tryin', Chief Officer – an' we're not lookin' for favours from Fean Island.'

He went back to his friends and they went away while Carrick headed up towards the village.

It might be election day in the Lochard constituency and a lot of political fortune might hang on the result. But Feanport's share of the excitement came down to two bored policemen standing outside the village hall on polling station duty, plus a solitary National Party supporter with a tartan rosette who was being watched by a large Alsatian dog which looked too tired to yawn.

Going in past the policemen, exchanging a nod with a

voter who was ambling out, Carrick found the polling booths were empty. The grey-haired woman with the modesty curtain in front of her table looked up hopefully, saw he wasn't a customer, and went back to reading her book. Milne Vullan was standing farther back, talking seriously to a young man who wore tweeds and a clerical collar.

A clatter of crockery guided Carrick to a side room. He went in and discovered Dorothy Vullan and Shona in a small kitchen, making coffee.

'Look what's turned up,' said Dorothy Vullan dryly. Like Shona, she was dressed in slacks and a sweater. 'Can we rise to an extra cup, Shona?'

'No way.' The girl wrinkled her nose at him in a mock disdain. 'Staff and friends only.'

'I qualify,' said Carrick sadly. 'I've drawn shore duty for the day.'

'Staff,' agreed Dorothy Vullan. 'Give him a cup.'

She turned as she spoke, brushing against the table. A large leather handbag lying at the edge tumbled, the contents spilling as it hit the floor.

'Damn,' said Dorothy Vullan and got down on her knees to gather them up.

Stooping to help her, Carrick retrieved a lipstick from under the table, handed it over, then reached under again and brought out a small, unlabelled bottle filled with small white tablets.

'Give me these.' Dorothy Vullan almost snatched the bottle from him. It disappeared back in her bag, then she gave him a slightly forced smile. 'Pain-killers, Chief Officer – for middle-aged muscles and creaky joints. Witchcraft by prescription, and I don't shout about it.'

They located the last of the handbag's contents then rose and Shona brought over two cups of coffee.

'What about Milne?' she asked. 'Will I take him one?'

'Wait till he's finished with the local church.' Dorothy Vullan glanced at Carrick. 'You've – well, heard about Lampeye?'

Carrick nodded.

'He didn't have family, so Milne wants to take care of the funeral arrangements.' She shook her head slowly. 'Poor Lampeye. I'm afraid it's easy enough to guess what happened.'

'John Marsh says he saw him near the harbour last night, early on, and he'd already had a few drinks,' volunteered

Shona sadly. 'He was an odd little man and he drank too much – but most people liked him.'

'I've heard worse obituaries,' said Carrick quietly. He turned to Dorothy Vullan. 'Is Marsh here too?'

'No, at the seaweed plant,' said Dorothy Vullan with a note of disinterest. She sipped her coffee for a moment then said suddenly, 'So Shona took you to the Clanstop last night. Did you enjoy it?'

'Yes.' Carrick met her green eyes and nodded calmly. 'What about your own evening? How was your friend?'

'Gossiping – as usual.' Her eyes held his own for a long moment as if probing, suspecting. Then she seemed to relax and shrugged. 'You said "shore duty". Does that mean you won't sail with *Marlin* on the ballet box run?'

'Captain Shannon doesn't believe in taking chances,' lied Carrick. 'He's leaving a berthing party for when he gets back in. Then we get those boxes up here.' He grinned. 'I'm not complaining.'

'He sounds as bad as Milne,' said Dorothy Vullan resignedly, setting down her cup. 'Milne says he'll stay on here until the island votes arrive. Still – come back up here once the polling stops, Chief Officer. It won't be much of a party, but I've more sandwiches, and a bottle or two of something stronger than coffee.' She saw Carrick hesitate and added dryly, 'Shona will be along too.'

'It's the best offer I've had,' said Shona maliciously.

He grinned, agreed, then watched Shona turn and collect her shoulder-bag, which had been lying on a chair.

'I'm meeting my father,' she explained. 'He wants me along with him when he sorts out the insurance claim form for the *Rachel* with the local agent.'

'Then take your wandering sailor when you go,' suggested Dorothy Vullan, pouring herself more coffee. 'I've enough problems.'

Carrick didn't argue. They said good-bye to the Witch of the Isles and left. Outside the hall, past the policemen, Shona gave a sigh as they walked along the street.

'There's one thing she didn't tell you,' she said quietly. 'She knows about that "Burn the Witch" slogan at the harbour – a damned fool of a cleaning woman told her first thing this morning. Milne knows too, and John Marsh. That's why the *Sea Whip* is berthed at the seaweed jetty again. She thought it would be better not to bring the boat into the harbour – not today, after Lampeye's death.'

'Nobody's blaming her for that,' said Shona gravely.

'She's expecting it,' countered Shona. Then she touched Carrick's arm and gestured ahead. Angus Grant was waiting at the next corner, a grim expression on his face. 'He's in a raw mood, Webb. Because of Lampeye – though he won't admit it.'

They reached Grant a moment later and the bearded fishing skipper greeted them with a nod.

'Got those insurance papers, girl?' he asked bluntly.

'In my bag,' she confirmed.

'Good.' He made an impatient noise. 'Then we'd better get along. I've a busy day – and a boat to work tonight.'

'Taking the *Duchess* out again?' queried Carrick.

'Aye, but trying further south,' said Grant flatly. 'There's a better chance o' decent fishing down there.'

Giving another curt nod as a farewell, Grant hustled Shona away. Left alone, Carrick stuck his hands in his pockets and watched them heading along the street for a moment. Then, with his own plans in mind, he set off in the opposite direction through the north end of the village towards the seaweed plant.

It took about ten minutes, then the low clutter of huts and the jetty appeared ahead and a moment later the distinctive, totally unmistakable odour of drying weed hit his nostrils. The smell grew stronger, almost overpowering, as he reached the wire fence which surrounded the plant and went in through the opened main gate.

He found the plant office, one of the nearest of the huts, and looked in. It held a couple of desks and some filing cabinets but it was deserted so he closed the door again and walked on, exploring as he went. Some of the huts were the equivalent of open barns, holding stacked bales of dried, compressed weed ready for shipment. Machinery was thudding somewhere near but there was still no sign of life.

Carrick turned towards the jetty. Great mounds of green, recently landed weed were stockpiled near it which meant the smell was even fiercer and the air thick with flies. The light breeze from the sea made things slightly easier once he reached the jetty and he walked out to where the *Sea Whip* was tied up. He called out, got no answer, and on an impulse stepped aboard.

The launch's for'ard cabin door was locked. It was the same when he tried the other cabin aft. Taking another glance round the deck, he shrugged and stepped back on the jetty again – to find John Marsh standing there, eyeing him quizzically. A few paces behind Marsh was another figure, a tall, thick-set workman who had a scowl on his face, a badly split lip and one eye blackened and almost closed.

'We keep her locked up, Carrick,' said Marsh casually, a faint amusement on his lined, sallow face. 'There's too much valuable laboratory gear installed aboard for Milne to want to take chances.'

'I had that notion.' Carrick thumbed at the burly figure beside the plant manager. 'Is that Campbell?'

'Who had – ah – a disagreement with your bo'sun?' Marsh nodded. 'But he's not the type to hold a grudge.'

Campbell managed a battered grin and shook his head.

'As fights go, I imagine you could have sold tickets for it,' mused Marsh. 'Still, that wouldn't bring you here.'

'I came looking for you,' said Carrick. 'Mainly to talk about Lampeye – the word is you saw him at the harbour last night.'

'Late on,' agreed Marsh. 'After he'd been thrown out of the Anchor Watch.' He paused and shrugged. 'I reckoned he'd just sleep it off, as usual.'

Campbell grunted agreement, scowled and said painfully, 'Shouldn't ha' happened. Stupid wee sod.'

'Campbell was a lodger at Lampeye's hut,' explained Marsh carefully. 'We've just been down there, but I'm afraid anything Lampeye left behind comes down to old clothes and empty bottles.' He shook his head sadly. 'You know, he didn't particularly like you, Carrick.'

'He didn't seem to like many people,' said Carrick softly. a small cloud of flies from the seaweed dumps buzzed around him for a moment, and he brushed them away. 'Did he say anything to you last night?'

'He ranted on,' shrugged Marsh. 'About the usual – how the MacLeans had done him out of his job with Angus Grant but that he'd get his own back on them. Nothing that – well, made sense.'

'Anything about who was stirring up things against Dorothy Vullan?'

Marsh frowned, turned, and jerked his head at Campbell, gave an unperturbed shrug and moved off.

'Well?' asked Carrick.

'No.' Marsh's thin mouth tightened. 'Carrick, there's more than one way to stir up this Witch of the Isles business. Trying to be helpful could be one of them. Milne

Vullan's an old friend – I think I can cope. Tonight, for instance. I'll be over here with him. But Campbell will be doing a stint as watchman over at Fean House.'

'He's big enough,' said Carrick dryly.

'Agreed.' Marsh considered him for a moment with an odd, almost sympathetic expression. 'Carrick, I'm leaving Feanport in a few days, heading south again. that won't upset Dorothy Vullan, I can tell you. It's time I moved and – well, Milne's fishing trials are over, he can cope with the weed plant till he gets someone else.'

'I'm more interested in their other problem,' said Carrick neutrally. 'How they're going to cope with the local "Burn the Witch" brigade.'

'That'll die off,' said Marsh confidently. 'Maybe not overnight, but with things back to normal – well, people have short memories.'

'In this part of the world?' Carrick was more than doubtful.

'I'll bet on it,' declared Marsh. Giving Carrick a friendly nod, he turned and walked away.

There was a guffawing, catcalling audience of fishermen on the quayside when Carrick returned to *Marlin*. The reason for their delighted amusement was in the water alongside the fishery cruiser – the patrol launch, coughing and spluttering and emitting occasional bursts of sick blue smoke while Clapper Bell and one of the deck hands bent over the engine with apparent puzzled concern. It travelled a few yards, spluttered, and stopped and drifted to more delighted comments from the quayside.

But as Carrick went aboard *Marlin* the petty officer on gangway duty winked at him. Captain Shannon had promised there would be a valid reason for leaving the patrol launch at Feanport and the pantomime was his answer.

He saw Shannon a little later, the latter wearing a clean white shirt and his best uniform and ready to go ashore on a final, formal visit to Milne Vullan as Returning Officer prior to the ballot box run. They talked briefly, Shannon's thoughts obviously on the immediate task he had ahead, then the fishery cruiser's commander set off at the same time as the patrol launch ignominiously spluttered in towards the quay, astern of *Marlin*, and tied up.

Clapper Bell's continued performance as the irate bo'sun lasted while he left the launch and returned aboard *Marlin*.

But as the quayside audience drifted away he relaxed and grinned at Carrick.

'Couple o' swopped-round plug leads was all it took,' he said cheerfully. 'Uh – the Old Man detailed Harris an' Edwards for tonight. Suit you?'

Carrick nodded. They were the same two experienced hands who had manned the patrol launch on the trammel net expedition. For once, Shannon was being as helpful as possible.

The afternoon drifted on and gave way to early evening. Shannon had been gone for about an hour when Malcolm Henderson's elderly sports car threaded its way down the harbour and stopped at the fishery cruiser's berth. The lanky detective inspector unfolded from behind the wheel, ambled aboard, and restricted himself to amiable noises until he was alone with Carrick in the wardroom. Then, slouched back in a chair, a drink in one hand, he explained why he had come.

'It's just a look-in, to bring you up to date – then I've got to go and sort out a domestic drama inland, a farmer who tried to feed his wife sheep-dip. The usual – their one and only shepherd was last seen scurrying off for the hills.' He paused and shrugged. 'The main thing I've got for you is the autopsy result on Lampeye. He had a skinful of liquor, like we guessed, and the official report says death by drowning.'

'But?' Carrick sensed there was more.

'The same again. Signs of a thump on the head, though it could have happened before or after he went in.' Henderson sighed despairingly. 'Any other time, and I'd have written it off. Right now – I'm damned if I know, but it'll have to wait.' He took a gulp from his drink. 'Feanport – hell, anyone who towed the place out to sea and scuttled it would be doing me a favour.'

'Did you run a check on Robert Chester, like I asked?' pressed Carrick.

'Uh-huh.' Henderson shaped a grimace. 'I telexed the London Metropolitan boys. They've no listing for any antique dealer of that name, but it means nothing – it seems plenty of these characters buy and sell without every really setting up shop.'

'The MacLeans?'

'Still zero – either they've been white as the driven snow or they've never been caught at anything. But' – Henderson leaned forward, nursing his glass, and shaped a conspiratorial grin – 'I've one little surprise for you. Remember you told me that Vullan and John Marsh were brother officers in the wartime navy?'

Carrick nodded, puzzled.

'I tried making the usual friendly noises about Marsh to the Ministry of Defence – how I'd be grateful for any information about this former officer.' The grin took on a lopsided edge. 'Ten minutes later I had a call from our Chief Constable, and got the deep-freeze treatment. A direct order to forget about friend Marsh and keep my mouth shut. Nice to have friends, isn't it?'

'You know what you're really saying?' asked Carrick, feeling as if the lanky figure opposite had just dropped a bomb on his lap.

'Me?' Henderson shook his head. 'No comment. But if you want to play guessing games –'

Carrick nodded. If John Marsh was under Ministry of Defence protection, it threw a totally new light on his role beside Milne Vullan – and on Vullan's sound fishing experiments.

He remembered how he'd felt when the ultrasonic effect had hit him in the water, the way it had twice blown sets of echo-sounding equipment, and the mad underwater stampede it had caused among marine life. Suddenly, with a startling clarity, he realized how the same effect, translated from what Vullan had termed 'small-scale trials' into larger scale possibilities, had possible major implications in terms of submarine weaponry.

Whatever Milne Vullan had set out to achieve. Even letting Vullan work away on his own, far away from any limelight, made security sense – and other things tied in too, from the way Department had told Shannon to mind his own business to John Marsh's declaration that now the trials were over he would soon be leaving.

'That's it, and I've got to move.' Finishing his drink, Henderson set down his glass, got to his feet and crossed to the wardroom door. Then he paused and glanced back. 'Just remember I didn't tell you, right? I've still four payments to make on the car, so I'd like to keep working.'

He left. Carrick was still standing in the wardroom, still slightly dazed at what he'd heard, when the little sports car growled away from the quay.

But, by the time Captain Shannon returned aboard a

little later, Carrick had decided one thing. He would say nothing to Shannon for the time being – and from the edgy mood in which that small, bearded figure began storming around the fishery cruiser it was the right decision. When he did tell Shannon the result of the post mortem, the sole response was a grunt.

Dusk arrived, to an accompaniment of renewed coughs and splutters from the patrol launch as Clapper Bell made a further brief show of trying to repair the engine. Then, a little later, as the grey became night and the moon appeared, a trickle of boats began to leave harbour for their night's work on the fishing grounds.

Leaning on a deck rail near the bow, Carrick watched them murmur past. One of the last to leave was the little *Duchess* with the tall, unmistakable figure of Angus Grant in the dimly lit wheelhouse, his face impassive as granite as he steered his borrowed charge past *Marlin*.

Turning away, leaving the rail, Carrick almost collided with the shadowy figure of Clapper Bell.

'All set, Clapper?' he asked absently.

Bell nodded. 'I've switched the leads back the way they should be on the patrol launch, sir. Uh – just one thing, when we're ashore. How about using the Anchor Watch as a base?'

'We're being left to do a job, not to organize some extra drinking time,' said Carrick stonily. Then he relented a little. 'I'll settle for you working a rota with Harris and Edwards. One man always down at the harbour, keeping an eye on the launch, the other two –'

'You'll know where we are an' we'll turn out fast enough,' promised Bell with a white-toothed grin and left him.

Marlin sailed on schedule, at 20.00 hours. Minutes before the harbour clock came round to eight p.m. Carrick went ashore with Bell and the two seamen. The gangway was hauled aboard, the fishery cruiser's twin diesels came to life moments later, the little group on the quayside cast off her mooring lines, and she edged out with a soft putter of exhaust from her squat funnel.

They waited until the slim grey shape, little more than a silhouette apart from her navigation lights, had cleared the breakwater entrance. Then they left, Harris drawing first watch on the launch, Bell and Edwards heading for the Anchor Watch, and Carrick for a stroll around the village.

A few late voters were still trickling into the polling station when he passed the village hall but otherwise the streets were quiet. On an impulse he walked from there to the seaweed plant but it was dark and deserted, the main gate padlocked. Feeling like a cop on the beat, he returned to the harbour, checked with Harris at the launch, and then headed for the Anchor Watch.

The bar was as busy as ever and Clapper Bell and Edwards had broken down the barriers enough to get into a darts match with a couple of fishermen. He watched till it finished and the sidebets were settled, bought Bell and Edwards a drink, then gossiped with them for a spell until Bell nudged Edwards and pointed towards the door.

The seaman went off to take his turn at the harbour. From the deceptively innocent expression on Bell's face, Carrick had the feeling that the bo'sun's turn down there would coincide with the Anchor Watch closing for the night. But it was nine-thirty, voting at the polling station had ended half an hour earlier, and it was time he got there.

'Any problems, an' we'll come and get you,' promised Bell then grinned. 'But I'm bettin' on a quiet night.'

It looked that way when Carrick reached the village hall. The door was closed, the two constables weren't in sight, and only the lights at the windows showed the hall was still occupied. He knocked at the door, and it was Shona Grant who opened it and let him in.

'If many more people turn up, it's going to be standing room only,' she said dryly, leading the way.

One glance around and he saw what she meant. With Milne Vullan as local Returning Officer, the polling station procedure at Feanport seemed to take a fairly elastic view of the rules now voting was over. There were about thirty people standing around gossiping and drinking coffee, including the two constables who had shed their tunics and were in an obvious off-duty mood.

'Good evening, Chief Officer. Come to join our little party?' beamed the elderly, grey-haired woman who had manned the polling table. 'Do you know, we had a sixty-eight per cent poll, a full two per cent higher than last time –'

He mumbled a polite reply then was rescued by Shona who piloted him through the other groups into the side-room kitchen he'd visited before, leaving most of the babble of conversation behind. Dorothy Vullan was there, presiding over a bubbling coffee urn while her husband sat back in a chair, his feet up on a table and a cigarette dangling between his lips.

'Hello, Carrick.' Milne Vullan grinned up at him without shifting his position. 'I heard *Marlin* got away on schedule. Well, all I've got to do now is wait till she gets back.'

'Captain on the bridge, stopwatch in hand,' said Dorothy Vullan tartly. Like Shona, she was still in sweater and slacks. 'Who's going to take another coffee pot out to that waiting horde?'

Chuckling, Shona took the waiting pot and went back out into the hall while Dorothy Vullan leaned against a counter, sighed and ran a hand over her short, copper-bronze hair.

'Take a break and put someone else to work,' suggested Carrick mildly. 'From the size of that mob outside, you've earned it.'

'I'd settle for a drink,' she declared. 'And I don't mean coffee – but there's nothing left.'

'Hold on till John Marsh gets back,' soothed Milne Vullan.

'Gets back?' She stared at him oddly. 'I thought – I thought he was still here.'

'I left a couple of spare bottles of gin on the *Sea Whip*,' said Vullan amiably. 'Just in case – he slid out about ten minutes ago to get them.'

'I see.' Dorothy Vullan turned away from them and fiddled with the coffee urn for a moment. Then suddenly, she faced them again. 'Milne, you should be out in the hall, circulating, making "thank you" noises.' Her lips tightened slightly at her husband's amused reaction. 'I mean it. Take Webb with you, introduce him to people. Move – I want to tidy in here

Looking slightly startled, Vullan got up and beckoned Carrick to follow.

'Never argue with a woman in a kitchen,' he said sadly, as they entered the hall. 'It's too damned dangerous.'

For the next few minutes, Vullan led Carrick around, introducing him to a variety of names and faces till he was called across to the other side of the hall and left Carrick talking to a farmer in leather-patched tweeds. Then Carrick saw Shona standing near, beckoning urgently. He escaped from the farmer and joined her.

'Something wrong?' he asked.

'I don't know.' She moistened her lips. 'I – it's Dorothy Vullan. She's gone –'

'What do you mean, gone?' Carrick asked quickly.

Shona shook her head, bewildered. 'I went back into the kitchen and she quizzed me about John Marsh – if I'd seen him leave, if he'd said anything. Then – well, she said she had to go out, that she wouldn't be long and I wasn't to tell Milne. I – there was something about her, Webb. Something I've never seen before.' The girl gripped his arm. 'It was as if she was frightened.'

Carrick swore under his breath. 'What about earlier on – how was she?'

'The usual, I suppose. Maybe slightly edgy, but she's been here helping Milne.' Her grey eyes met Carrick's anxiously. 'Webb, I just have a feeling –'

'That makes two of us,' said Carrick softly. 'All right, just get me out of this place quietly.'

'I'll get us both out,' she retorted. 'I'm coming along too.'

He nodded, knowing arguing wouldn't have done much good. Easing through the chatter and laughter, they reached the hall door and slipped out. Pausing, Carrick glanced up and down the empty, darkened street and thought of Clapper Bell at the Anchor Watch. Then he shrugged. That might be wasting time, and he still didn't know what was happening.

'If John Marsh was going to the *Sea Whip* –' Began Shona.

'We'll head there too,' he agreed.

They set off through the village, Carrick setting a fast pace and the girl having to move at a near trot to keep up with his longer stride. Only a few people were out and about, none paid them any attention, and at last the dark, jumbled outline of the seaweed plant showed ahead. It still seemed in total darkness but as they reached the outer fence Carrick gave a soft grunt of satisfaction. The previously padlocked gate lay slightly open.

'Somebody's still here,' he said quietly. 'All right, so we go in and look. But that's all.'

She nodded and they went into the plant yard, skirting the black shapes of the storage huts. Shona caught Carrick's arm and pointed. The door of the office hut lay open, light streaming out of it.

They walked towards the door then stopped dead, a low moan of disbelief coming from Shona. They had found the

Witch of the Isles. Dorothy Vullan was on her knees in the centre of the brightly lit office, bending over the sprawled, motionless figure of John Marsh.

Shona moved first, darting forward, and Carrick followed. As they entered the hut, Dorothy Vullan looked round at them with a haggard despair on her face – and at the same instant the door was kicked shut behind them.

'Thanks, Mrs Vullan,' said a sardonic voice. 'Now all your friends have to do is stay peaceful.'

Carrick turned slowly to meet the mocking face of Lachie MacLean and the double-barrelled menace of the shotgun the stockily built fisherman held in a rock-steady grip.

'Get over beside her,' ordered MacLean. 'Move.'

Powerless, they obeyed. Bending over Marsh, Carrick saw that he was unconscious but still alive – and winced at the ugly, broken welt across the man's scalp, a welt which still had blood oozing along its edges. He glanced up at Dorothy Vullan, who was standing gripping Shona's hand.

'I'm sorry,' said the Witch of the Isles in a dull, listless voice. 'It's my fault, all my fault, but –'

She stopped there as the hut door was flung open. The man who came in was Robert Chester but the alleged antique dealer was dressed in a fisherman's jersey and slacks and his thin face was a cold, calculating mask.

'You shouldn't have stuck your nose in, Carrick,' he said almost sadly. 'You or the girl – and I had a man watching the gate.'

'Another of the MacLeans?' asked Carrick bitterly.

Chester nodded, glanced around the office, and shrugged. 'I didn't expect any of this. But we can cope.' He turned to Lachie MacLean. 'Another five minutes should do it. Just keep them here and keep them quiet.'

Shona Grant had been staring at the two men, total, shocked bewilderment on her face. She took a half-step forward, ignoring the menace of the shotgun.

'If the MacLeans are here, what have you done with my father?' she asked desperately. 'They –'

'Your father's aboard the *Duchess*, making a one-man fishing trip,' said Chester, cutting her short. He thumbed at Dorothy Vullan. 'Ask her. She knows.'

He went out, closing the door. Moving over, Lachie MacLean leaned against it in a way that was relaxed but watchful, the shotgun held steady. Wide-eyed, still bewildered, Shona turned desperately to Dorothy Vullan.

'He said you know.' She gripped the older woman by the arm. 'What is it, Dorothy? You've got to tell me.'

'It shouldn't have involved any of you,' said Dorothy Vullan wearily. 'None of this was meant to happen –'

'But it has,' said Carrick grimly. He heard MacLean give a coarse chuckle, but ignored the man. 'Do I make a guess at it to save time? That the Witch of the Isles did a deal to sell out her husband's ultrasonic work – and that Chester is stripping everything he needs from the *Sea Whip* right now?'

'Yes.' The word came like a sad whisper from Dorothy Vullan. She saw the shocked disbelief on Shona's face and added quietly, 'Your father was helping me, Shona. He – well, he understood.' She managed an attempt at a smile. 'Angus Grant isn't an easy man to convince. But he agreed – and all the rest between us lately has been play-acting?'

'Play-acting?' The girl moistened her lips and pointed to Marsh lying on the floor. 'Is that what you call it?'

'I didn't know he'd come here tonight,' said Dorothy Vullan earnestly. 'It shouldn't have happened. As soon as I heard, I – I tried to go after him and stop him.' Bitterly, she looked at Lachie MacLean. 'But I was too late.'

'What did you expect when he came chargin' in?' queried MacLean, unperturbed. He eased the shotgun against his hip and gave Carrick a fractional grin. 'Hell, the old biddy still thinks the boss is just buyin' a new fishing gimmick.'

It didn't seem to register with Dorothy Vullan and Shona was still in the same state of almost complete bewilderment. Carrick drew a deep breath, knowing they hadn't much time, certain he had to find out more because it was likely to decide what lay ahead for them.

'You've a right to know – now.' She clenched her fists and looked down at them, her voice low and far away. 'Just over six months ago, two things happened at the same time. Milne turned down an offer from a European fishing combine who wanted his sound fishing system and – and I got the results of a hospital test he didn't know about.'

Something in the way she said it made Carrick understand.

'Those pills?'

She nodded.

'How long?' he asked gently.

'Under a year, they said.' She made it sound unemotional. 'You could call me lucky. When it happens, it'll be quick – I'd hate to be one of those long-time-a-dying people. But you see, I had to do something, for Milne. That's when I got the idea.'

Carrick glanced at Shona and saw she was listening intently, the shock and bitterness gone from her, their place taken by a guarded compassion. Even MacLean, standing guard as before, had wiped the grin from his face.

'Tell us about it,' encouraged Carrick. 'Go on.'

'Milne wouldn't know how to earn a living any ordinary way,' said Dorothy Vullan with a wry attempt at humour. 'He – well, he works on his own and doesn't even try to understand about money. And forget those stories you'll hear – the Witch of the Isles hasn't any fortune tucked away. There are things like death duties. He'd have to sell Fean House, and afterwards –' she shook her head. 'I decided I wasn't going to let that happen.'

She stopped there, bending quickly over Marsh as the man stirred a little and groaned. But it ended at that, and she rose again slowly, sighing.

'You said you went to my father,' reminded Shona. 'Why?'

'That was later.' Dorothy Vullan moistened her lips, choosing her words. 'First, I – well, I decided what to do. Milne was determined not to sell the sound fishing process, or whatever you'd call it – even though he said he'd talked to our own fisheries people and they weren't particularly interested. But I knew about the offer, and I knew it would still be open.'

Carrick swallowed hard. 'So you contacted them –'

'Yes. One of their people had read an article by Milne in some scientific journal. He hadn't spelled out what he was doing, but they'd guessed. They – well, they agreed it could be done my way, offered me a hundred thousand pounds, and sent Robert Chester to see me. We planned a way.' She turned to Shona. 'That's when your father came into it. I needed him.'

'I'd have thought he was the last person,' declared Carrick, wondering how much longer it would be before Chester returned.

'He was the very first – maybe the only one,' said Dorothy Vullan firmly and glanced at Shona. 'Angus Grant and I understand each other – and I told him everything. There was going to be a hate stirred up against the Witch – I knew that wouldn't be too hard. We needed a boat and

Chester needed his own people in Feanport. Well, that wasn't so easy. But when Angus agreed that meant we had his boat. Then he brought the MacLeans in as his new crew. At least' – her eyes strayed to the man at the door – 'that's the name they call themselves, whoever they really are.'

Lachie MacLean shrugged but didn't answer.

'And tonight?' pressed Carrick.

'Seemed the ideal night,' she said sadly. 'Everyone busy with the election – while some unknown fishermen with a spite against the Witch would steal the *Sea Whip* and –'

She stopped there, as the office door was flung open again. Chester came in, gave them one glance, then nodded to MacLean.

'Move them out,' he said curtly. 'We'll take them with us. I want clear of here before anyone else shows up.' A flicker of tension crossed his thin face. 'Carrick, you and the girl bring Marsh. You come too, Mrs Vullan – and don't waste my time arguing.'

'Where are you taking us?' asked Shona tightly.

'A boat trip, so you'll be less of an embarrassment.' He dragged a small automatic from his pocket. 'Now move.'

They left the office hut in a small procession, Chester first gripping Dorothy Vullan by the arm. Carrick and Shona followed, carrying the limp weight of John Marsh between them, and Lachie MacLean brought up the rear prodding them along with the shotgun. Chester led them through the dark shadows of the huts to the jetty, and the figures of the other two MacLeans appeared out of the night on the *Sea Whip*'s deck.

'Get aboard.' Chester shoved Dorothy Vullan across as he spoke. As she stumbled on the deck, Carrick and Shona were prodded after her, still carrying Marsh.

Carrick saw a rubber boat with an outboard engine lying on the launch's deck near the bow. Some plastic wrapped packages were piled together in the cockpit, mere shapes in the faint glow of the binnacle lights.

'Aft,' ordered Chester. 'Donnie, you and Lachie shove them in the cabin. Willie, start her up and cast off –'

'Tell me something,' said Carrick grimly. 'Who are you working for, Chester?'

'People who pay good money – on delivery.' Chester twisted him a humourless grin in the darkness. 'I don't need to know how this gear works, just get it to them.'

'And what about anyone who gets in the way – like a village cop or a little drunk like Lampeye?'

Chester's face was a harsh, mask-like silhouette in the night for a moment. Then Lachie MacLean dug Carrick viciously with the shotgun and hustled them off. They carried Marsh in after Dorothy Vullan through a low, narrow doorway into the inky blackness of the after cabin, the door slammed shut, and they heard a bolt slap into place.

'Find a bunk,' said Carrick, as he heard Marsh give a new, sighing moan. 'Shona –'

'To your left,' she told him.

Almost blindly, with only a faint trace of moonlight coming through the cabin's tiny portholes, Carrick let her guide him, then between them they laid their burden on one of the cabin's bunks. Dorothy Vullan had been clicking light switches, but they didn't work.

'There's a torch somewhere,' she declared, and began feeling her way around the cabin, colliding with Carrick in the process. 'At least, there was –'

'Chester would check.' He stopped her and guided her over to sit on the bunk on the other side, bringing Shona over too. At the same time, the *Sea Whip*'s engines began to murmur and footsteps hurried along her deck. 'Finish what you were telling me back in the cabin. What was the rest of the plan?'

'To take the launch out into the middle of the bay, then set her on fire,' said Dorothy Vullan tiredly. 'That way –'

'That way, she'd blow up when the fuel tanks caught – while they got clear away in the rubber boat, with the ultrasonic gear,' nodded Carrick. 'Then what?'

'They'd rendezvous with Angus Grant, land Chester down the coast – and Angus would sail back into Feanport from a night's fishing with a full crew.' She paused as the *Sea Whip*'s engine note changed and the cabin took on a gentle sway. They were starting to move. Then, making a strained effort to keep her voice under control, she added, 'These crates Chester has on the dockside are full of rubbish, not antiques. Milne's equipment would go in them and nobody would think twice when they were moved south.'

Marsh was groaning again, his limbs twitching. But Carrick listened for a moment to the *Sea Whip*'s engines as the launch nosed away from the shore. Chester was keeping her speed to a crawl.

'So what do you think they'll do with us?' he asked bluntly.

'Land us somewhere,' suggested Shona hopefully.

'No chance,' he told them. 'There's a slogan on the harbour wall – Burn the Witch. That's all they've got to do. Just leave us locked in here, and when the launch goes up that's the problem solved.'

'They couldn't,' protested Dorothy Vullan.

'They killed George MacKenzie and Lampeye.' Carrick hardly paused to let her digest that. 'You may have thought you were selling a load of new-style fishing gear, but it's something a damned sight more important, whatever your husband told you. And John Marsh isn't just a friend who overstayed his welcome – as far as I know, he's Ministry of Defence, here to keep an eye on what was going on.'

'Oh God,' she said in a low, trembling voice. 'But – there's Angus Grant –'

'So they get rid of him too,' he said brutally. 'Which means only one thing matters now – that we get out of this.'

'How?' asked Shona.

'How about witchcraft?' he said sardonically. 'The only way out is that damned door.'

They stared at each other, Carrick with a feeling of total helplessness.

'You're wrong,' said Dorothy Vullan simply, making them swing round. 'It looks that way, but you're wrong. Milne altered all sorts of things aboard – and he took five feet off the rear of this cabin to make a special battery compartment.'

Carrick moistened his lips. 'Can we get into it?'

She nodded in the darkness. 'The rear panel is on clips. Then there's a hatch that will take you out on deck. But –'

The murmur of the engines increased a shade and the *Sea Whip* lurched as she answered her helm. Carrick peered out one of the tiny portholes and saw the lights of Feanport twinkling. They were already a good distance from shore. Once they get out beyond the middle of the bay any time left might come down to seconds.

'Help me,' he said quietly. 'We haven't much time.'

The rear panel was a single sheet of plywood and came off easily, then Carrick squeezed through into the battery compartment, felt his way past the racked batteries which fed Milne Vullan's experimental gear, and found the hatch.

Easing it open a fraction, he took a deep breath of salt air then looked around.

The stern of the launch was deserted. One man was in the cockpit, at the helm, another was working at the rubber boat near the bow, and a faint glow of light from the for'ard cabin showed where the other two must be.

Opening the hatch wider, he wriggled out and crawled along the deck. He could hear the man in the cockpit whistling to himself as he steered. It was Lachie MacLean, and the binnacle lights showed the man's shotgun propped beside him.

Quietly, Carrick reached the door of the aft cabin, slid the bolt, felt the door push open from within, and murmured a warning. Then, on hands and knees, he crawled towards the cockpit and the unsuspecting helmsman.

A small brass fire extinguisher was clipped to the rear of the cockpit combing. Crouching, Carrick gauged his distance, then sprang. As he landed in the cockpit he grabbed the fire extinguisher, pulled it free, then as the startled helmsman swung round, mouth opening, Carrick brought the fire extinguisher down hard on the man's head.

He caught Lachie MacLean as he fell, lowered him to the deck, then realized the steering wheel was spinning loose. Cursing, he grabbed for it – at the same time as the *Sea Whip* lurched and a frantic shout came from the man at the bow.

A moment later, Chester erupted out of the for'ard cabin with Donnie MacLean hard on his heels. Hurling the fire extinguisher at them, Carrick swung round to reach for the shotgun. He didn't make it. The automatic in Chester's hand barked, a fierce lance of pain ripped into Carrick as the bullet slammed into him high, near the shoulder, and he felt himself falling.

But someone else was suddenly in the cockpit beside him, seizing the shotgun, bringing it up in a single movement. On his knees, Carrick looked up in a daze and saw the tall, commanding figure of the Witch of the Isles.

The gun in Chester's hand barked again. Dorothy Vullan seemed to smile, to grow taller, surrounded by a strange power and purpose.

The shotgun in her hands slammed its first barrel and Robert Chester uttered a strange half-scream as he spun on his feet like an agonized doll and vanished over the side.

She fired again, precisely, unhurriedly. Framed in the light of the for'ard cabin doorway, a fuel can in his hands, Donnie MacLean gave a high-pitched screech and fell backwards.

The man at the bow had frozen where he was, hands raised in surrender, as Carrick hauled himself back on his feet. The Witch of the Isles didn't help him. Still strangely tall and remote, she was staring at the for'ard cabin.

Little tongues of flame were appearing. In a moment, they were bigger, then a roaring mass of fire. Carrick saw a smile on her face and clutched at her.

'Get out,' he croaked. 'Shona and Marsh –'

Then, when he took his hand away from her, he saw it was covered in blood. His blood or her blood, he wasn't sure which. He saw the man at the bow dive overboard and start to swim. Swallowing at the pain it caused him, he dragged a groaning, stirring Lachie MacLean upright in the cockpit and switched off the *Sea Whip*'s engines. As the throb died and the launch began drifting he heaved MacLean over the side.

Dorothy Vullan was already at the after cabin door. Shona was there, the racing flames making the scene bright as daylight while she dragged John Marsh along the deck towards a liferaft container.

Moving in a half-dream, half-nightmare, singed by the heat and flames, Carrick helped them release the liferaft. It inflated with a whoosh as it hit the water. Then they half-fell, half-tumbled aboard, dragging Marsh with them, and pushed away from the burning hull.

Shona had the liferaft's paddles. He took one, she used the other, and they struggled to get further away from the floating inferno. At last, they stopped, and Carrick looked at her, nodded, and felt a new wave of weakness coming over him.

Marsh was lying at their feet, moaning again. Dorothy Vullan was sitting upright, staring at the night. He touched her, and the arm which had been resting on the raft's side fell limp, fingers brushing the water.

A white-cored blast came from the *Sea Whip* as her fuel tanks exploded. He felt the hot wind of the explosion against his face . . . and the darkness that followed was deeper than the night.

It was two days later, when he was sitting up in bed in

Feanport's cottage hospital, that Carrick heard the final verdict in it all.

He'd had earlier visitors, earlier conversations which had helped him put most of it together. How the flames had brought the patrol launch hammering out from Feanport to find the liferaft – and to pick up Willie and Lachie Maclean from the water.

John Marsh would live. He'd been operated on for a fractured skull, but was recovering. The same surgeon had later removed the bullet from Carrick's shoulder, with grunts about what would have happened if the wound had been a couple of inches lower and to the right.

But there was nothing anyone could do for the Witch of the Isles, and Carrick's version of what had happened was greeted with sympathetic scepticism.

'You see,' the same surgeon had said patiently. 'The bullet had penetrated the left ventricle of the heart. There is such a thing as volitional movement, but I'd say the odds are thousands to one she should have died instantly, so –'

Carrick hadn't argued. He knew, while police uniforms and Malcolm Henderson came and went, while Captain Shannon bustled around in a grim-faced way, and particularly when Milne Vullan came in, stood beside him silently, then quietly went out again.

But there was a different mood about Captain James Shannon when he entered Carrick's hospital room on that second day. Grunting, he plumped himself down in a chair by the bedside, tossed a bundle of magazines on the covers, then surreptitiously slipped a whisky flask under the pillow.

'That's from Clapper Bell,' he said gruffly, 'I've got to do everybody's dirty work. All right, how are you feeling?'

'Reasonable.' Carrick eased his bandaged shoulder. 'Another few days –'

'I heard.' Shannon dismissed the subject.

'Well, we're tidying it up. The two MacLeans are talking – they killed MacKenzie because of the way he was sniffing around. Lampeye was different – he was making too much noise about them. And on it goes.' He stopped and shrugged. 'The real problem is Angus Grant, and what the hell do we do with him. He didn't know about the killings, he only sailed a boat up and down, and Milne Vullan won't have him touched. That's the way it's likely to stay.'

'Good,' said Carrick softly. 'You know why he helped?'

Shannon nodded.

Carrick had heard it from Shona, the previous evening. Dorothy Vullan had told her in the desperate moments while they'd waited in the cabin and Carrick had been out on deck.

There had been several reasons. But the one which had mattered was that Dorothy Vullan had only one blood relation. Shona would be the next Witch of the Isles – and the eventual owner of Fean House.

'So' – Shannon broke the silence with a heavy throat-clearing – 'What's left isn't much, except for a couple of things. I've talked to Vullan about this ultrasonic thing. Frequencies, harmonics, amplifiers, God knows what. The Ministry of Defence boys swooped on him after that paper, and hit him over the head with the Official Secrets Act. He went to work for them, with Marsh as resident guard-dog, like you thought.'

'And what happens to it now?' asked Carrick grimly.

'Now?' Shannon's bearded face twisted in a sardonic grin. 'Nothing – because the series of final tests proved it doesn't work anywhere except around that damned Witch-rock area. Something about underwater rock formations, acoustic echoes – hell I didn't even try to understand.' He saw Carrick's expression, and nodded. 'Marsh was going down to London to tell his bosses to forget it – that's the irony of the whole mess.'

Unable to think of anything to say, Carrick watched him get to his feet. Shannon crossed to the window, looked out for a moment, then came back.

'I said a couple of things. The other is this –' he paused, scratching his beard. 'Now we've finished that damned election duty, *Marlin*'s going back on normal patrol. We'll be working the Barra Head area for a couple of weeks. Then we'll come back to Feanport, and collect you. Understood?'

'Understood,' said Carrick softly.

Shannon gave him a surprising wink, turned, and went out.

Carrick lay back and for the first time in two days he smiled. He had another visitor due. They had things to forget, things to remember.

But two weeks was plenty of time . . . even for a brand-new Witch.